SINISTER HOUSE
& OTHER STORIES

Whispering Beeches stands vacant, well back from the roadway, almost hidden by the thickly growing trees that give it its name — though since its owner, Doctor Shard, was murdered by an unknown hand three years ago, it has locally been known as Sinister House. One night, noticing a light in one room, newspaper reporter Anthony Gale enters through the open front door — only to stumble over a man's body lying stark and rigid, with a gaping throat wound! Four tales of mystery and the macabre from veteran writer Gerald Verner.

GERALD VERNER

---◆---

SINISTER HOUSE
& OTHER STORIES

Complete and Unabridged

LINFORD
Leicester

First published in Great Britain

First Linford Edition
published 2015

A catalogue record for this book is available
from the British Library.

ISBN 978–1–4448–2665–4

Published by
F. A. Thorpe (Publishing)
Anstey, Leicestershire

Set by Words & Graphics Ltd.
Anstey, Leicestershire
Printed and bound in Great Britain by
T. J. International Ltd., Padstow, Cornwall

This book is printed on acid-free paper

To the memory of P.M. Haydon

Sinister House

1

The Empty House

Psychologists have stated that the human brain is incapable of holding two troubles at the same time and giving an equal amount of attention to each. The greater worry will invariably overcome the lesser, and Anthony Gale, as he strode savagely along the deserted and dimly lighted road crossing Wimbledon Common, would have been the first to admit the truth of this — if he had thought about it at all, which he did not. His mind was far too fully occupied with his recent quarrel with Mollie to allow room for profound truths to creep in, and he was also in a very bad temper, which is not the ideal state for any man who wishes to indulge in sane and consecutive thought.

So angry was he that for the first time during the past three weeks he had totally forgotten the fact that he was out of work and with no immediate prospect of finding a job, the opportunities offered to little-known freelance journalists with a predilection for crime stories being few and far between. Women were unreasonable, thoroughly unreasonable, he thought angrily. After all, he had only asked Mollie a simple question. There was no need for her to have flown into a temper, and what had she been doing, anyway, on the previous evening with Louis Savini in Shaftesbury Avenue?

Anthony disapproved of Savini. Any decent fellow would disapprove of a man who was known to be a crook and a blackmailer and something worse, associating with the girl to whom he was practically engaged. Besides, Mollie had deliberately lied to him. He had gone to considerable trouble in getting two seats for the new show at the Orpheum because she had said she wanted to see it — luckily the manager was a friend of his; funds did not permit him buying expensive theatre tickets — and at the last moment, just as he had been preparing to dress, she had phoned up to say that she'd got such a bad headache that she was going to bed, and would he excuse her?

Anthony had been duly sympathetic — he remembered bitterly some of the extravagant things he had said — and had spent a most boring evening sitting beside an empty seat watching one of the worst plays he had ever seen. It was only the fact that the seats had been given to him that had prevented his walking out after the first act.

It had been purely an accident that he had seen Mollie at all. There had been a traffic block, and while he was waiting to cross the street to catch his bus she had come out of the Trocadero, looking radiantly beautiful in a new evening dress, and accompanied by — Anthony ground his teeth — Louis Savini! They had got into a waiting taxi and driven off before he had had time to recover from his first shock of surprise.

After spending a wakeful night and considerably more tuppences than he could afford in trying to ring the girl up, Anthony had hurried round to her flat at the first available opportunity, only to be told that she was out.

Cooling one's heels for over five hours and a half on the corner of a busy street is not the ideal method by which to prepare for a delicate interview, and Anthony felt the strain.

He communicated some of this in his manner when he did eventually meet the girl, and his greeting, if not exactly cold, was certainly lacking in that carefree joyousness which Mollie appeared to expect. His subsequent remarks, too, were the reverse of tactful. There were several things he called Savini without once mentioning the word 'gentleman', and Mollie retaliated — with her own private opinion of men in general and Anthony in particular, concluding with a fervent wish that she might never see him again, and following this up with a strategic movement that left him gazing stupidly at the polished front door that had just been slammed in his face.

All these things considered, Anthony felt, as he walked homeward with long angry strides, that he had just cause for thinking that women were unreasonable.

There was, too, a dull heavy ache somewhere inside him, and an insane longing, that was anything but pleasant, to get out of himself so that he could not think. What could there be in common between a girl like Mollie Trayne and an oily crook of Savini's calibre? he wondered miserably. Until chance had opened his eyes, he had never even known that they were acquainted, and Mollie had flatly refused to offer any explanation for her inexplicable behaviour.

Anthony strode on savagely, kicking at the loose stones on the surface of the rough road, his brain dizzy and aching from the chaotic whirl that revolved ceaselessly about one central, fixed idea. Mollie had turned him down for a slimy creature in whose veins was such a mixture of nationalities that it would have been impossible to extradite him without dividing him into four quarters! Anthony at that moment would have cheerfully undertaken such a congenial task. He was conscious of a horrible sense of blankness — or something terribly vital to his existence that had been destroyed, and deep within him a hopelessness that was almost unbearable.

He lived in a tiny cottage on the outskirts of Roehampton, and there was no necessity for him to have come this roundabout way home, except that he felt he wanted exercise and a longing for space and air. The cottage was his own freehold — it had been left him, together with a small legacy, by an aunt two years before — and that was Anthony's only excuse for living so far off the beaten track.

He came eventually to the end of the common, crossed over a broad road and struck off again, skirting the corner of Putney Heath. His sense of direction was entirely mechanical, but he was well acquainted with every inch of the neighbourhood, and could have found his way blindfold.

Presently he swung into a wide avenue that led through to within a hundred yards of his small demesne. It was lined on either side by large houses, each standing in its own considerable acreage of ground. Most of them, as Anthony knew well, were empty and neglected, relics of a past prosperity awaiting demolition by the jerry-builders and the erection of 'modern desirable residences' in their stead.

There was one house, about halfway down the avenue that had always interested him because of the history that attached to it. Grim and silent, with sightless staring windows. Whispering Beeches stood well back from the roadway, almost hidden in the thickly-growing trees that surrounded it and gave it its name. And its reputation in the neighbourhood was as grim as the house itself, for a tragedy had taken place within that dark and gloomy pile three years previously which had earned it the name of Sinister House. The figure of Death had stalked abroad there, its scythe red with the blood of a murdered man. Since the fatal night when Doctor Shard had been struck down by an unknown hand in his laboratory, the house had remained empty, and had the reputation of being haunted.

There were stories in circulation of

shadowy figures seen after nightfall flitting about the weed-choked grounds and of lights flashing behind the dark windows.

Anthony believed none of these stories, but from sheer idle curiosity and because the place fascinated him, he had made a habit of stopping every time he passed the house at nightfall and looking at its black bulk, dimly visible at the end of the long drive. He had never seen anything, but it had become almost second nature with him, and tonight, although his mind was elsewhere, the habit asserted itself and he paused for a second by the broken gate. Almost unconsciously he surveyed the house, and as he looked he suddenly drew in his breath with a sharp hiss.

In one of the lower rooms a light gleamed! Anthony Gale concluded that his imagination was playing tricks with him. He closed his eyes quickly and opened them again, expecting to find that he had made a mistake, and that the house would be in darkness. But the light was still there, faint and dim like a will-o'-the-wisp. Then, as he continued to

10

gaze steadily at the window from which it came, a dark something passed in front of it, and an instant later it went out!

All the journalist in Anthony came uppermost. For a moment he forgot his quarrel with Mollie, forgot everything except that he had stumbled on the possibility of a story. Without hesitation he began to make his way up the dark drive, avoiding the gravel and keeping to the grass borders. Long neglected by shears and mower it was thick and rank, and completely deadened his footsteps so that he advanced noiselessly to where a huge yew tree grew in front of the main entrance. In the shadow of the massive trunk, Anthony paused and listened.

The night was very still and, save for the faint rustle of the leaves as the topmost branches of the beech trees stirred softly in the faint breeze, there was not a sound. What was the explanation for that light? Obviously there was someone about in the deserted house, and Anthony was determined to find out who, and what they were doing.

He crept forward stealthily until he

reached the steps leading up to the shadowy porch. Here he saw something that the darkness had prevented him from seeing before. The front door was open! He felt a thrill of excitement run through his veins. Who was inside, and why?

Without a sound he tiptoed up the worn, moss-grown steps and noiselessly entered the pitch-black hall, pausing again to listen as he crossed the threshold. This time he thought he detected a slight sound, an almost inaudible sibilant sigh that seemed to come from somewhere on his right.

Anthony felt the hair on the back of his neck prickle. There was something altogether horrible about that sigh from the darkness. He waited motionless and rigid, but there was no repetition of the sound, and after a minute he began to move forward slowly. The room in which the light had been was on the right of the front door, and he stretched out his hand and felt along the wall on that side of the hall, until presently his groping fingers came in contact with the frame of a door. He felt round this, and touched nothing but empty air. The door was apparently open.

Anthony advanced cautiously, and as he did so an overpowering sense of being watched took possession of him. The presence as of somebody behind him — out in the black vastness of the hall! He took two more steps forward, and almost cried out as he stumbled over something that lay on the floor — something that was soft and yielding! He put out both hands instinctively to save himself, fell on his knees, and touched something wet and sticky!

With a sharp cry of horror he recoiled and, pulling out a box of matches from his pocket, struck a light. In the feeble yellow glimmer he saw that he had fallen over the body of a man — a man who lay stark and rigid, with a gaping wound in his throat. But it was the white, terror-distorted features that held Anthony's gaze. For it was the face of Louis Savini!

2

The Man in the Dark!

Louis Savini!

There was no mistaking that dark, sallow face, in spite of the fact that the thick over-red lips were twisted back in a grin of agony and terror.

Anthony felt a curious, cold sensation creep down his spine as the match he was holding flared up suddenly and died down, and at the same time from behind came the faint creak of a disturbed floorboard, the almost inaudible shuffle of a step! He remembered the feeling of an unseen presence, and swung round, the dying match burning his fingers. A figure, black, shapeless, was creeping towards him from the open door! A crouching deformed-looking shape, with two white, talon-like hands, outstretched, crooked and clutching before it! Anthony felt a wave of terror such as he had never experienced before steal over him at the sight of those long, slim ivory hands, and then the match went out!

The blackness after even that feeble glimmer was intense, and the silence that followed indescribably horrible. It seemed as if the whole universe suddenly stood still, and then out of the darkness came a rustle, the faint swirl of silk-like garments, and the next second something launched itself at Anthony, and he was fighting desperately to keep those bony fingers from his throat!

A shudder went through him as the clawing hands of his unknown adversary touched the skin of his face and neck, for they were cold with the coldness of some-thing long since dead; the uncanny chill of death itself! And yet behind their grip was an enormous strength, a strength that taxed his muscles to the utmost as he strained to free himself from that strangling grasp. One skinny hand had fastened on his throat, and the twining fingers were tightening, tightening, causing the blood to thunder to his brain.

Exerting all his force, Anthony wrenched

madly at a thin, steel-like wrist, but without avail. The hold about his neck never loosened a fraction of an inch. Great purple and orange lights flashed before his eyes, and he felt his senses reeling. A few more seconds and he knew that he would lose consciousness. With a supreme effort he succeeded in freeing his right hand from the clutch of the other, and struck out blindly. He heard a faint gasp of pain, and for an instant the choking grip relaxed. He staggered back two paces, drawing in great gulps of air hoarsely and painfully, tripped over the body of the dead man, and fell heavily to the floor. Before he could even attempt to struggle to his feet, his unseen assailant was on him, and again he felt those horrible hands seeking for his throat. If once they got a second grip, Anthony knew that he was done for. Grasping the fleshless wrists of his attacker, he strove to keep those eager fingers away from his neck, but slowly and surely the other gained ground.

Anthony's aching muscles cracked under the strain, but his arms were being gradually forced up. The unknown man in the dark seemed possessed of almost in-human strength. Anthony could feel his hot breath fanning his cheek, but no sound escaped him, and there was something horrible, uncanny in that very fact, that silent remorseless struggle for mastery.

At last, with a shock that sent a convulsive movement through his limbs, he felt the icy touch of those death-like fingers on his chin; another moment and they would be at his throat! With a sudden jerk he twisted his body to one side, still grimly holding on to the other's wrists. Over and over they rolled across the floor, and eventually Anthony found himself uppermost. His advantage, how-ever, was short-lived, for his opponent was as slippery as an eel. Wrenching his hands free, he suddenly gripped Anthony round the back of his neck, at the same time thrusting both his knees upwards sharply. Anthony turned a complete somersault over the other's head, and landed with a crash on his back. His head struck the floor with terrific force, and to the accompaniment of myriad darting lights he lost consciousness!

* * *

His first impression as his senses slowly
returned to him was that his usually
comfortable bed had, in some manner,
developed an unaccustomed hardness.
Every bone in his body ached, and his
temples seemed to contain an imprisoned
steam-hammer that was trying its utmost
to burst its way through his brain. With
a groan, he pressed his hands to his
forehead and sat up. The movement
caused the agonizing pain in his head to
increase, but after a moment this abated
slightly.

He was in pitch darkness, except for a
dim square of dark blue to his right, and
as his mind gradually cleared, he
remembered his discovery of the dead
body of Savini and his fight with the
unknown man in the dark. Apparently he
was still in the empty house. After waiting
for a moment to let the pain in his
temples subside, Anthony struggled shak-
ily to his feet, feeling in his pockets for his
matches. They were not there and he
remembered having dropped the box in

his shock on first discovering Savini. He felt about on the floor, and presently found them. The box had been crushed underfoot during the struggle and its contents scattered, but luckily it still held three matches. Anthony struck one and, as it flared into life, he looked about him. He failed to suppress the involuntary cry of amazement that escaped him when his eyes went to the spot where the dead man had been, for — the body of Louis Savini had vanished!

Anthony stared stupidly at the bare floor, unable to believe his own eyes. Surely he could not have imagined the whole thing? His fingers strayed to his throat tenderly. He certainly hadn't imagined the fight in the dark — the pain in his head and the soreness of his neck were proof enough that that had been no dream creation! The match in his fingers went out and he struck another, bending down to examine the floor. No, there was no room for doubt. There on the bare boards was a large, sinister, irregular stain. He looked at his hands. They too were bloodstained. Savini *had* been murdered, but for some reason his body had been removed while Anthony had been unconscious.

He struck his third match, and, looking round the bare room, and saw the end of a candle stuck on the corner of the marble mantelpiece. It must have been the light from that, he concluded, that had at first attracted his attention. He went over and lighted it. As he did so, he saw propped up against the wall behind it an envelope. Some writing was scrawled across it in pencil and, bending nearer as the candlelight grew stronger, Anthony with something akin to a shock made out his own name! The writer evidently knew him!

He tore open the flap and extracted the contents, a single sheet of cheap note-paper. Written on it, in the same sprawling hand as the address on the envelope, was the following:

* * *

'You will be sensible if you forget everything that you have seen tonight. I could have killed you as easily as I killed Savini, and shall not hesitate to do so if you become a nuisance. You escaped with your life merely because you know nothing. Where ignorance is life, it is folly to be wise.'

★   ★   ★

That was all. There was no signature. Anthony pursed up his lips in a silent whistle as he put the warning in his pocket thoughtfully. He had stumbled into a veritable maze of mystery. What a 'story'! A front-page story with banner headlines:

'MIDNIGHT MURDER IN EMPTY HOUSE! HISTORY REPEATS ITSELF IN SINISTER MANSION AT ROEHAMPTON.'

There was not a news editor in Fleet Street who would not welcome him with open arms; it was a big scoop. The biggest that had ever come his way. Anthony made up his mind to take it to the *Courier*. He had done several odd jobs for Downer, and he might possibly get a commission to cover the affair. He glanced at his watch. It was half-past one. If he hurried straight away, and was lucky enough to get hold of a taxi, he would be in time to do a write-up for the morning edition. They'd hold up the presses for a story like this — an exclusive.

He took a hasty look round the bare and dilapidated room to see if there was anything that would give him a clue to the identity of the man who had attacked him — the murderer of Savini. But there was nothing and, picking up the end of the candle, he turned to depart. Making his way out into the wide hall, he was about to open the front door, which was now closed, when a faint sound from the shadows of the big staircase startled him and made him swing round hurriedly.

A dark heap of something lay at the foot of one of the massive banisters, and as he looked it stirred slightly, and a smothered moan reached his ears. Holding the candle above his head, Anthony approached cautiously and bent down.

And here he received the third and

greatest shock of that night of surprises, for the dark heap was revealed as the figure of a woman, and the wide eyes that stared up at him from the ashen face were the wide eyes of Mollie Trayne!

3

The Night Intruder

Anthony hastily stuck the candle on the ledge of the lower stair and dropped on his knees beside the girl. 'Mollie!' he exclaimed, blank astonishment in his voice. 'What on earth are you doing here?'

She looked at him vacantly for a moment, her eyes dull and lustreless. Then she struggled up on his supporting arm. A faint whiff came to his nostrils as she moved, a sickly-sweet smell that left no doubt in his mind as to the cause of her present state. The girl was recovering from the effects of a drug. She had been chloroformed!

'Tony!' She breathed the name almost inaudibly. 'Tony, what happened? I — I feel dreadfully sick!' Her voice trailed on incoherently.

'You'll feel worse if you try to move,' he replied as she made an effort to rise. 'Lie still for a moment and the sickness will wear off.'

She sank back against his arm and passed a trembling hand over her eyes. For a few moments she lay motionless, with closed lids, while Anthony watched her anxiously, puzzling his brains as to the meaning of this fresh development. What was Mollie doing at the sinister house at this hour of the morning? Evidently she had been attacked by the same mysterious person who had fought with him in the dark, but what had brought her there in the first place? Had she come with Savini? Anthony went cold at the thought. If she had, unless she had been drugged beforehand, she must have been a witness to the murder!

Presently she opened her eyes and he saw that they had recovered something of their brightness.

'Feel better now?' he asked gently, and she nodded.

'Yes, thank you,' she replied.

'Tell me what happened,' said Anthony, helping her sit up.

'I don't know,' she answered. 'I only

remember getting as far as the front door, and then somebody caught me by the shoulders and before I could move or cry out something was pressed over my face, and I don't remember any more.'

'But what brought you here? Why did you come?' demanded Anthony.

Mollie rose unsteadily to her feet, clutching at his arm for support. 'I — I can't tell you that,' she said in a low shaky voice.' She swayed so badly that Anthony had to slip his arm round her waist to keep her from falling.

'You'd better sit down again for a moment,' he advised. He tried to lead her over to the stairs, but Mollie shook her head.

'No, no,' she whispered, glancing around her with terrified eyes. 'Let me get away from this horrible place. It frightens me!' She took a faltering step towards the door.

'So you won't tell me what you came here for?' he persisted.

'I can't,' she repeated, and her voice sounded stronger and held a note of finality in it.

'Did you come with Savini?' asked Anthony sharply. He felt her fingers tighten on his arm at the question.

'No,' she replied slowly, 'I didn't come with Mr. Savini.'

'I suppose,' went on Anthony sarcastically, 'that you had no idea he was here?'

'Yes!' She breathed the words so softly that he could scarcely catch what she said. 'Yes, I knew that he was here!'

'And that was the reason you came?'

'Partly.' The answer was a long time coming, as though it were being forced out of her against her will.

'I see,' said Anthony bitterly. 'You needn't trouble to explain any further.'

'You don't see!' she cried sharply. 'You don't see at all!'

'I think I do,' he retorted, and then with that odd unaccountable desire which comes to people to hurt the ones they love most, he added: 'Anyway, you'll never be able to meet Savini again. He's dead!'

'Dead!' she gasped. 'Not — not murdered?'

A wave of contrition for the unnecessary bluntness of his remark swept over

Anthony. 'I'm sorry,' he muttered. 'I shouldn't have told you like that. I — '

'But you must — you must tell me!' she interrupted, grasping the lapels of his coat with both hands. 'You must tell me everything! How did it happen? Where?'

He remained silent, wondering why she had jumped so quickly to the conclusion that it had been murder.

She waited a moment and then, as he did not reply, she continued in a husky whisper: 'Was it — here?' Anthony nodded. 'Murdered!' She looked fearfully about her with terror in her eyes as she murmured the ominous word.

'I didn't say he was murdered,' said Anthony, watching her covertly. 'I only said he was dead.'

She raised her eyes to his face inquiringly but it was in shadow, and she could see nothing of its expression. 'Wasn't he — ' She stopped, leaving the sentence unfinished.

'He was, as a matter of fact,' Anthony admitted. 'But what made you think so?'

'I — I don't know — I just thought — ' she stammered vaguely, and the hand on his arm trembled violently. Then suddenly she burst out: 'Oh, let us go — let us go!' She ran to the door and began to fumble with the latch desperately, glancing back over her shoulder with wide eyes.

Anthony followed, carrying the candle in his hand, and as he passed the open door of the room where Savini had met his death, his foot kicked against some small object that lay on the floor. He stooped quickly and picked it up. It was a little leather case, and without waiting to give it more than a cursory glance, he hastily slipped it into his pocket. Mollie's attention had been taken up with the fastenings of the front door, and she had failed to notice his action.

As he reached her side she managed to twist back the catch, and stepped out into the darkness of the porch.

'If we can find a taxi, I'll take you home,' he said as she hurried down the steps and half-walking, half-running, made her way quickly along the weed-grown drive.

'You needn't bother — I've got a car,' she answered breathlessly.

'Got a car!' he echoed in astonishment.

'Yes, I left it round the corner — in a side street.'

Anthony flung away the still-lighted end of the candle that he had been carrying and gripped her arm. 'Look here, Mollie!' he exclaimed sternly. 'You're hiding something. What do you know about this business?'

She did not attempt to pull away from him, or even deny his statement, but remained silent.

'You must have come here for some reason,' he continued. 'What was it?'

'It's no good asking me, Tony,' she said after further silence, and there was a hint of impatience in her voice. 'I've said once that I can't tell you, and I mean it.'

'But — ' he began, and she interrupted him.

'You don't understand, and it's better that you shouldn't try,' she spoke rapidly and nervously. 'Forget all about tonight, and what happened in that horrible house as quickly as you can. It's got nothing to do with you, and you'll be wise if you take my advice.'

They had reached the gate by now, and passing through, she stopped on the pavement. 'Ring me up tomorrow — in the afternoon,' she went on. 'And remember what I've said.' She squeezed his arm, and before he could speak or stop her, was running swiftly down the deserted avenue.

For a moment Anthony felt inclined to follow her and demand an explanation of her strange words, and then realizing the futility of it, he shrugged his shoulders and looked undecidedly about him. A clock somewhere in the distance struck two sonorous strokes and warned him of the lateness of the hour. Even if he were lucky enough to pick up a belated cab, which was extremely unlikely, it would be useless going to the offices of the *Courier* now. He wouldn't get there until nearly three if he started at once, and by the time he had written his copy it would be too late anyway for the morning editions.

He made up his mind to go home, and see Downer first thing in the morning. With this intention he turned and swung off in the opposite direction to that taken by Mollie, covering the ground at a good pace.

He occupied the short walk to his cottage in reviewing the mysterious events of the evening, and trying vainly to account for Mollie's extraordinary behaviour, and the reasons for her presence at Whispering Beeches. The whole thing, from the murder of Louis Savini onwards, was inexplicable — a nightmare — and Anthony felt his tired brain reel dizzily as he tried to grapple with it. He arrived at his cottage, let himself in, switching on the light in the tiny dining room, mixed himself a stiff whisky-and-soda and drank it at a gulp.

His aimless wanderings of the evening and the excitement that had followed had made him feel dead tired, and he was in his bedroom and partly undressed before he remembered with a start the little leather case he had picked up in the hall of the empty house.

Reaching over for his jacket, he took it from his pocket. It was a flat pouch-like affair of pliable leather, fastened with a catch button, and remarkably old. There was something hard inside, and Anthony knew it was a key before he put in his finger and took it out, with a slip of paper.

The key had obviously been made to fit a patent lock, for it was shaped something like a Yale, though only half the size. Anthony examined the paper that had accompanied it. It bore several jumbled lines of letters and figures and was evidently either a code or the key to a code. The paper was old; the lettering in ink that had already begun to fade.

Anthony searched the case carefully for a further clue, but there was none, nor did it bear any markings. He decided to examine it more closely in the morning and, replacing the key and the paper, slipped it under his mattress, and with a weary yawn continued his undressing. His head had hardly touched the pillow before he was asleep.

A faint sound from somewhere near at hand woke him instantly and he sat up in bed. The room was in darkness, but outside the door and immediately opposite was a landing window which overlooked the little garden at the back, and there was enough light in the sky to show him that his door was opening slowly! He watched, listening intently, and presently heard somebody breathing softly. The door swung wider, and now he could see silhouetted dimly against the grey square of the window beyond, the vague shadowy figure that was stealthily entering!

Anthony silently stretched out his hand towards a small electric torch he kept on the table beside his bed and without removing his eyes from that sinister creeping shape, closed his fingers round it. A loose board creaked and at the sound, Anthony sprang out of bed and flashed on his lamp.

He caught a glimpse of a black figure crouched to spring; saw the lowered head enveloped in a bag-like mask; and then something struck him on the shoulder so violently that he dropped the torch, and in another second was grappling with the intruder.

His right hand touched something cold; he felt a sharp pain shoot up his arm, and his fingers became wet and sticky. He guessed that it was a knife that the night visitant carried, and lashed out wildly. He heard a smothered gasp and a clatter as something fell to the floor; then he received a kick on the shin that sent him stumbling to his knees, a door slammed, and the key turned in the lock.

Anthony staggered to his feet and, limping across to the light switch, pressed it down. The room was empty. The intruder had gone, leaving behind him as a souvenir of his presence the long-bladed, black-handled knife that glittered evilly on the floor!

Anthony had to break open the door before he could make his way to the bathroom and bathe and bandage the deep cut on the back of his hand, which was bleeding profusely. It was during this operation that he suddenly realized the object of the burglary. The visitor of the night had been seeking the leather wallet that he had picked up in the hall of the empty house!

4

The Green Car

All desire for further sleep had left him and, having attended to his wound, Anthony made his way downstairs. The first pale streaks of dawn were filtering in through the windows of the dining room and, glancing at the clock on the mantelpiece, he saw that it was half-past four. He also saw something else. The drawers of the sideboard had been pulled out and their contents scattered in a heap on the carpet.

With a grim little smile tightening the corners of his mouth, Anthony explored further and found, as he had expected, that every room in the cottage had been subjected to a methodical and rigorous search. Evidently the intruder had exhausted all other possibilities before turning his attention to the bedroom, for even the kitchen and the hall-stand had not escaped him.

His means of gaining admittance had been through a window in the microscopic scullery, for Anthony found the neat circle of glass that had been cut out to enable his hand to raise the catch, lying on the sill. Whatever secret the key and the slip of paper contained it was obviously of considerable value to the unknown person or persons behind this mysterious business. Anthony examined his rifled home carefully to see if he could find any clue to the identity of the masked burglar, but there was nothing.

Putting on a kettle, he washed and shaved, dressed himself, made some tea and, carrying this into his small study at the back, went upstairs and fetched the leather case. Sitting down at his disordered writing-table, he withdrew the contents and, laying them on the blotting pad, stared at them with wrinkled brows.

There was nothing to be learned from the key. It was of brass, and the maker's name had been carefully scraped off, apparently with a file. Anthony put it aside and turned his attention to the scrap of paper that had accompanied it, but although he puzzled his brains for nearly an hour, he could make nothing of the jumbled rows of figures and letters that covered it. At last he drew a sheet of paper towards him and made a careful copy of the aged document — for aged it undoubtedly was.

The lines of figures and letters ran:

'M.O.C. V.2.P.101. L4. W.5. L.6. W.8. P.116. L.2. W7-9. L20. W7. L.45. W6-9. L30. W.1. P.120. L.10. W.3. L4. W5-6. P121. L19. W7-9.'

Having completed his copy, Anthony put the key and the original back in the wallet and slipped it into his hip pocket. Then, with a writing-pad and pencil before him, he tried every known form of deciphering the cryptogram. It was seven o'clock before he finally gave it up in despair and, lifting the cover from his battered typewriter, began to bang out an account of his adventures of the previous night.

He read it through with pride when he had finished, and justly so, for it was a good story and lacked none of those elements so dear to the heart of a news editor — and so rare. Putting it in his pocket, Anthony found that there was just time to boil himself an egg before setting off for the resplendent offices that housed the brains and pulsing heart of the *Courier*.

Mr. Downer, that greatly harassed and pessimistically minded man whose blue pencil had succeeded in breaking the hearts of more reporters than any other news editor in the Street, listened to what he had to say and read the closely typed sheets without visible sign of interest. Reaching the end, he turned a weary and faded blue eye on Anthony — he had a habit of keeping the right permanently closed, and nobody could ever remember having seen both Mr. Downer's eyes open together.

'This is all right,' he said dispassionately. 'Wait a minute.' He picked up a pencil, scribbled an illegible scrawl across the top of the copy, slashed through half a dozen lines and, stretching out his hand, rang a bell.

'Take that to Mr. Short,' he barked,

throwing the manuscript to the boy who answered the summons, and Anthony saw his story whisked away to the sub-editor.

'I've told Short to splash it — front page — banner headlines,' remarked Mr. Downer, helping himself to a cigarette. 'You'd better notify the police. There should be some further developments. Cover the affair, and let me know!' He drew a slip of paper towards him and scrawled his name on it. 'Take this to the cashier for expenses. Goodbye!' Without looking up, he began to search among the pile of papers littering his broad desk. Anthony, who knew Mr. Downer rather well, and was therefore undismayed by the abrupt termination of the interview, picked up the slip he had thrown across to him and left the office with a grin.

Strolling along the passage, he made his way to the reporters' room and, nodding to the solitary occupant — a red-headed man, who was industriously scribbling away at a desk in one corner — he picked up the telephone, and within a few minutes was talking to an interested official at Scotland Yard. The conversation was lengthy, but apparently highly satisfactory, for Anthony's face still bore its cheerful smile when he finally hung up the receiver.

'You seem to have struck something,' remarked the red-haired, man looking up from his labours. 'Couldn't help hearing what you said. Sounds interesting.'

'It is,' agreed Anthony. 'What are you doing, Smith?'

Castleton Smith made a grimace of disgust. 'Writing up yesterday's dog show,' he said lugubriously. 'About as exciting as Tooting on a wet Sunday! All I know about dogs is that one end barks and the other doesn't!'

Anthony chuckled, and the other regarded him enviously.

'I wish I was doing your job,' he remarked. 'It's always been my ambition to run up against a real juicy murder.'

'Every dog has his day,' said Anthony sententiously, and slammed the door to avoid the heavy directory that the exasperated Smith hurled at him.

He had reached the big vestibule of the offices before a thought suddenly struck him, and he retraced his steps towards a room on the second floor. Here were housed huge files containing back numbers of the *Courier* from the time when that enterprising journal first saw the light of day. After a ten-minute search Anthony found what he wanted, and presently became engrossed in an account of the murder of Dr. Shard, the original owner of Whispering Beeches. Shorn of the embellishments supplied by the fertile imagination of the reporter who had covered the case, the details were, briefly, as follows:

Four years ago there had arrived, quietly and unheralded, from America, a middle-aged, retiring, rather shy man who had bought Whispering Beeches and settled down there with a small staff of servants. It soon leaked out that this unassuming personage was none other than Dr. Emanuel Shard, the famous cancer specialist, whose research into the cause and cure of the dread disease were world-famous.

Immediately the house was besieged by reporters anxious to obtain an interview with the great man, but Dr. Shard refused to see any of them. He sent a message by his secretary and assistant — a man named Caryll — stating briefly that he was engaged in experiments concerning a cure for cancer, that he had chosen the house for the sake of its quietness, and didn't wish to be disturbed in his labours.

A year went by, during which Shard lived practically the life of a hermit, and his very existence was forgotten. And then one morning Duson, who combined the roles of butler, housekeeper, and general factotum for Shard, and who was eccentric and refused to have any women servants round him, found his master lying dead in his big laboratory at the back of his house, a knife buried to the hilt between his shoulder blades.

Recovering from his first horror at the discovery, Duson went to wake Caryll, but the secretary's bed had not been slept in, and he was nowhere in the house. The police were called in and a description of the missing man was circulated throughout the country, but without result. He had apparently vanished into thin air.

Whether he had been the murderer or not was a matter for conjecture, for there was no clue to show the motive for the crime. Nothing had been stolen, and no one had heard any quarrel between Shard and his assistant — in fact, the evidence showed that they were on the very best of terms.

The sensational crime had faded into the background, and finally became relegated to the limbo of forgotten things — one of those unsolved mysteries, remembered vaguely by the public, and worked on patiently by certain men who sit in a grim building overlooking the Thames Embankment. Such was the pith of the case, and when he had finished reading the various reports, Anthony Gale rose to his feet and left the offices of the *Courier* with a feeling of disappointment.

What it was he had expected to find he couldn't have said, but it had certainly occurred to him that this three-year-old crime might have had some bearing on the recent events in which he had become involved, and possibly thrown a light on the meaning of the cryptogram and the key.

The thought of the key turned his steps westwards. The unknown person or persons who killed Savini were obviously anxious to get it, and it would be just as well if it were placed beyond their reach. Anthony had an account at the Union and Southern Bank — so microscopic these days as to be barely noticeable, but still an account — and calling in, he put the flat leather case and its contents into an envelope, sealed it, and handed it over to be given up only on his personal application.

He experienced a sense of relief when he had done this, for the possession of that wallet, he was convinced, was a source of danger. His lack of sleep on the previous night was beginning to have its effect. He felt terribly tired and weary, and he was debating in his mind the advisability of returning to his cottage for a rest, when he became aware of a car that was moving slowly along in his wake.

There was nothing particularly extraordinary in this, except that Anthony was certain that he had seen it before that morning. It was a two-seater coupé painted a dull green, and on the long radiator there was a peculiarly shaped mascot — a tiny silver model of the Statue of Liberty. He remembered having seen it outside the *Courier* offices as he had come out, and again when he had left the bank. Someone was trailing him!

He stepped on the edge of the sidewalk and waited for the car to draw level, hoping to get a glimpse of the occupant as it went by. But in this he failed, for evidently becoming aware of his interest, the driver suddenly pressed on the accelerator, and the car shot forward, flashing past him and disappearing round the next turning without his being able to get more than a blurred impression of the muffled figure crouching behind the steering wheel. But still he had learned something. His movements were being carefully watched, and he had little doubt as to the reason. His foresight in lodging the key at his bank was justified.

On his way to the station to catch his train home he called into Scotland Yard, but the man he wanted to see was out and not expected in until the following morning. Anthony scribbled a message for him and left, looking sharply about him as he emerged from under the big arch onto the Embankment. But though there was a stream of traffic passing in both directions, he could see no sign of the green coupé. The unknown trailer had apparently taken fright and given up the chase.

Anthony caught his train by the fraction of a minute, and so tired was he that he fell asleep and almost passed his station. It was with a feeling of intense satisfaction that he presently came to the gate of his cottage and paused, fumbling in his pocket for his latchkey. He had just taken out the bunch when he heard the whirr of wheels behind him, and turning saw the green car flash by and go speeding up the road!

He smiled grimly as he walked up the little pathway to the front door. These people, whoever they were, did not mean to let him out of their sight, even though they must know that the thing they sought was no longer in his possession. Or didn't they know? Perhaps they hadn't connected his visit to the bank with the leather pouch and its mysterious contents.

Anthony inserted his key in the lock, opened the door and, nearly reeling with weariness, entered the small lobby beyond. The next moment he was wide awake and staring with horror at the scene before him. The hall was in a state of the utmost disorder. A chair was overturned, and the rugs lay crumpled up in a chaotic heap. But it was neither of these things that caused Anthony to rub his eyes and look again, wondering if he were dreaming. It was the man who was sprawled in the middle of this confusion, for he was a complete stranger — and he was dead!

5

The Hooded Man

The light had gone from the sky, and the street lamps were beginning to assert their dim brilliance, when a man descended from a big limousine car outside Lambeth North tube station, spoke a word to the neatly uniformed chauffeur, and strode rapidly away towards Westminster. Passing the wide opening leading up to Waterloo, he dived down a narrow side turning, quickly traversed the dingy street, and swung round into another even meaner and dirtier than the first.

Halfway along this cul-de-sac — a high brick wall barred all exit from the other end — the man paused and, glancing swiftly about him, took a key from the pocket of his heavy coat and, approaching a grimy blistered door, unlocked it and entered. His feet thudded hollowly on the bare boards of the narrow, evil-smelling

49

passage beyond as, after closing the outer door, he made his way through to the back and unlocked a second door.

He stood looking out of this for a moment into the semi-darkness of a rubbish-littered wharf and listened to the faint lapping of water as the river brushed softly against the supporting piles. Then, closing the door but leaving it unlocked, he went back to the passage and slowly mounted a flight of creaking, rickety stairs to the first floor.

Entering a room on the right of the landing, he felt for and clicked down the electric light switch, flooding the place with a soft light and, crossing over to a wall cupboard, took out something which he proceeded to adjust carefully about his face. It was a hood of black silk, and into the eyepieces had been let squares of fine gauze which enabled the wearer to see without even his eyes being visible.

The room was sparsely furnished, a table and three chairs being all that it contained besides the cupboard, which hung near the bare mantelpiece. The windows were covered with shields of some tightly stretched black material so carefully fitted that not a vestige of light could creep past.

The masked man shut the door and locked it, and then, seating himself at the table, drew some papers from his pocket and began to read. To judge from the appearance of his hands, he must have been well past middle age, for they were wrinkled and claw-like, the pallid, ivory-coloured skin stretched taut over the bony knuckles.

For some time he sat motionless, perusing the pile of documents in front of him. Then suddenly, as a sound reached his ears from below, he gathered them up and returned them to his pocket.

There came the noise of a stumbling step on the stairs, and then, after a short pause, three taps on the door. The man in the mask rose silently from the table and went over, listening with his ear close to the panels. 'Who is that?' he asked in a low voice.

'Selton,' was the hoarse reply. Apparently satisfied, the unknown unlocked and opened the door.

A man entered hurriedly, blinking in the light, and the door was closed and re-locked behind him. The newcomer was short and dressed in a shabby suit of what had once been blue serge, but was now of a neutral colour, stained and shapeless. His face was long and unshaven, and from his left cheek to the point of his chin ran the diagonal scar of an old knife wound. It twisted the corner of his mouth, giving him a perpetual sardonic leer.

'Why didn't you come in more quietly?' snapped the masked man, returning to his seat at the table. 'Do you want to advertise our presence to the whole neighbourhood?'

'I can't see in the dark,' snarled the other, flinging himself down in a chair and pulling out a paper packet of cheap cigarettes. 'And them stairs are narrow.'

His companion regarded him critically. 'You're drunk,' he said coldly. 'And when you're drunk you're a fool, Selton.'

'Maybe I am,' growled Selton. 'Maybe I'm going to be drunker.' He lit his cigarette with a shaking hand. 'Lacy's dead!' he burst out suddenly.

The masked man gave a slight start. 'Dead!' he echoed. 'How did that happen?'

'They cut his throat,' said Selton, and his hoarse voice trembled. 'That nosey reporter caught him last night while he was trying to find the key. Lacy waited until he went out this morning and returned to the cottage for another look. I waited outside to keep watch in case this fellow Gale, or whatever his name is, came back unexpected. After two hours, and Lacy hadn't come out, I wondered what was up, and went to look for him.'

He paused and passed a shaking hand across his forehead, which was dewed with beads of perspiration. 'I found him all right — in the 'all, stone dead!' He shivered.

'Did they get the key?' asked the masked man, leaning forward.

'How the blazes do I know what they got?' cried Selton roughly. 'They got Lacy, and that's enough for me!' He brought his clenched fist down on the table with a bang. 'I'm through! I'm not taking any more risks, not if there was an 'undred million in it.'

'You're rattled,' said the other contemptuously.

'Perhaps I am,' snarled Selton. 'And so would you be, if you'd seen what they done to Lacy. I'm goin' to quit, and if you've got any sense you'll do the same!'

'I shall do nothing of the kind,' snapped the masked man. 'There's a fortune waiting for someone in that house, and I'm going to get it!' He drummed on the table with the tips of his repellent-looking fingers. 'I wonder if they found the key?' he murmured thoughtfully.

'I don't care whether they did or not,' grunted Selton truculently. 'If you hadn't made a mess of things last night and dropped it after you'd taken it from Savini we might 'ave got away with it. As it is, Lacy's dead, and I'm finished. I ain't going to have nothing more to do with it!' He glared across the table with bloodshot eyes. 'Give me some money, and I'll go!'

'You'll do no such thing,' growled the masked man. 'Or if you do you'll get no money from me.'

'Oh, won't I?' Selton leapt to his feet and stood swaying unsteadily. 'We'll see about that. You think I don't know who you are. You think all this mask business has taken me in. Well, it hasn't! I know you all right, you old devil!' He staggered forward and gripped the edge of the table, his face thrust close to the other's. 'And if you don't pay me I'll squeal. Do you hear — I'll squeal!'

The masked man remained motionless, his eyes glaring behind the gauzed slits.

'So you'll squeal, will you?' he said softly. 'Selton, you're a fool to threaten me!

'And I'll tell you something else,' screamed Selton, half-mad with rage and drink. 'That girl — you thought she'd come with Savini, didn't you? Well, she hadn't. She followed Savini, and I know just why — see! I saw her this afternoon talkin' to someone. Do you know who it was? It was — ' He lowered his voice, and almost whispered a name.

'Are you sure?' There was a note of alarm in the masked man's voice, and hearing it, Selton chuckled. 'Now who's rattled?' he taunted. 'Yes, I'm sure, and I don't blame you for gettin' the wind up. You didn't suspect she was in with them, did you?' he broke off, and held out his hand. 'Come on,' he continued harshly. 'I want some money, and I want it quick!'

'I haven't any with me,' answered the other. 'Come back here tomorrow at this time and I'll have some waiting for you!'

'I want it now,' said Selton with drunken obstinacy. 'I ain't coming here any more. If you haven't got it on you I'll come with you to get it!'

There was a moment's silence, and then: 'All right,' said the hooded man shortly. 'Wait a moment!'

He rose, took off the black silk hood, unlocked the door and held it open. 'Come on!' he said, and Selton passed out reluctantly into the blackness of the landing. He heard a click behind him as the unknown switched off the light, and cursed as his feet stumbled on the first stair.

It was the last sound he ever uttered, for at that moment there came a dull 'Plop — plop!' Two spears of flame stabbed the darkness and, with a choking cry, Selton went sliding down the stairs to lie crumpled at the bottom, an inert mass!

6

Enter Mr. Budd

The big-faced man who sat smoking a big cigar in Anthony Gale's little sitting room early on the morning following his discovery of the dead man in the hall might, from his appearance, have been put down as a prosperous farmer or a retired shopkeeper — in fact, anything but what he was; for Superintendent Robert Budd, known to his friends and enemies alike by the sobriquet the Rosebud, was as far removed from the popular conception of a detective as a Ford from a Rolls-Royce.

He was large and fat and lethargic; slow of movement. He never walked when it was possible to ride and never rode when it was possible to remain still. A veritable mountain of a man whose bulk overflowed the chair on which he sat, so that it seemed doubtful if he would ever be able to extricate himself from its embrace. And yet his brain was alert and, in contrast to his body, moved swiftly, for there was not a cleverer detective in the whole of Scotland Yard than this bovine, red-faced man, who listened silently while Anthony poured out the story of the mysterious happenings that had suddenly come into his life.

'Very interestin',' murmured Mr. Budd, gazing thoughtfully with a fishy eye at his evenly burning cigar, 'very interestin' indeed. I wish I'd been in when you called at the Yard yesterday, but I got the day off and went to a flower show.' Horticulture was the big man's hobby, and it was partly for this reason that he had earned his nickname. There was a story told with great relish by the assistant commissioner of how the superintendent had once spent four hours discussing the relative beauties of dog roses and orchids with Pritchard, the Dorking murderer, before he finally remembered that he had come to arrest the man and executed the warrant that reposed in his pocket.

'Yes, I wish I'd been in yesterday,' he continued with a sigh, 'but the flowers were lovely. They had a new tea rose there — '

'I'm not interested in roses,' broke in Anthony, cutting short his reminiscences. 'Let's stick to the matter in hand!'

The Rosebud looked at him reproachfully. 'All right,' he said wearily. 'They told me all about the murder at Whispering Beeches. Sergeant Wiles went down directly after you phoned and had a look round, but he found nothing except the bloodstains on the floor. Most of the other rooms in the house were locked.'

'I know that,' said the reporter. 'Wiles came over to see me afterwards and questioned me for an hour just after I'd found that poor fellow in the hall!' He nodded towards the door and shivered. Even now he remembered the horror of that moment.

'You mean Lacy,' remarked Mr. Budd, expelling a cloud of smoke, and Anthony looked astonished.

'Was that his name?' he asked.

'That was his name,' replied the

superintendent. 'We've got his record and compared the fingerprints. He was a pretty tough customer, too — been convicted three times for robbery with violence. I wonder what he was doing there.'

'I believe he was the same man who broke in on the night I found Savini's body,' declared Anthony. 'There was a big bruise on the side of his face showing the marks of knuckles, and I hit him pretty hard,' he added with satisfaction.

'Maybe,' agreed Mr. Budd, nodding his head ponderously. 'You think he came back again after you'd gone, to have another look for that wallet?'

'Yes,' said Anthony.

'I believe you're right.' The superintendent nodded again. 'But the question is who killed him, and why?'

Anthony made a gesture of despair. 'Ask me another,' he exclaimed. 'Who killed Savini? And why are they so anxious to get hold of that key and the paper?'

'And why should they kill the man who was sent to look for it?' interrupted the

61

big man softly. 'Was he killed because he had failed, or was he killed because they thought he had succeeded, or was he killed — ' He broke off abruptly. 'I'd like to have a look at that key and the cryptogram.'

'I'll get it,' said Anthony. 'We can go up to my bankers now if you like.'

The Rosebud shook his head. 'There's no need for all that hurry,' he said. 'Tomorrow'll do.' He paused. 'I was thinkin' of going along to have a look at Whispering Beeches,' he went on. 'I've got the keys of the place from Tallents, Shard's solicitors. They tell me that most of the furniture's still there, same as when the old man was killed. That was a peculiar case. I was in charge of it — not that that made it peculiar. It was peculiar because we never found Caryll. There's no doubt that he killed the old chap, though nobody knows why. It's funny that the same sort of thing should have happened there again, isn't it?'

'Remarkably amusing,' said Anthony sarcastically. 'I find it difficult to refrain from laughing!'

'They've put me in charge of this case, too,' went on the superintendent, ignoring the interruption. 'I asked them if they'd let me handle it, and they did.'

'Why were you so keen?' inquired the reporter, struck by something in his tone.

'Because I always expected something else to happen at that house,' said Mr. Budd, pulling steadily at his cigar, his heavy lids half-closed. 'I've been expecting it for three years. You know the name it's got? Sinister House — and that's what it is, sinister.'

He crushed out the stub of his cigar, and with an effort hoisted himself out of the chair. 'I'm going there now. I thought perhaps you'd like to come with me,' he said, pulling down his crumpled waistcoat. 'That's one of the reasons why I called here first.'

'What do you expect to find?' asked Anthony curiously, and the big man shrugged his massive shoulders.

'Everythin' and nothin',' he answered vaguely. 'What is it these other people expect to find? Cobwebs, dust?' He shook his head. 'There's something in that house so valuable,' he continued, 'that a murder more or less doesn't count if it helps to get it. And it's been there for three years.'

'Budd,' said Anthony seriously, 'I believe you know more about this business than you've said.'

The superintendent's fat face creased into innumerable wrinkles. 'Or perhaps I've said more than I know,' he retorted softly. 'Come along, let's go!'

They walked down the garden path to where an ancient two-seater car was waiting, and Mr. Budd, with some difficulty, squeezed himself into the seat behind the wheel.

Anthony had known the stout superintendent when he had walked a beat as a uniformed inspector, and before the C.I.D. had recognized his extraordinary capabilities. Between himself and the elder man existed a friendship that was all the more sincere because they seldom met, except casually, and then sometimes not for months at a time.

Anthony had kept Mollie's connection with the affair to himself, though he had been tempted several times that morning to take the Rosebud into his confidence. But second thoughts had prevailed, and he had kept silent. He was infernally worried about the woman. On the previous afternoon he had rung her up, as she had suggested, only to be informed that she was out; and on each successive occasion — eight in all — he had been given the same message. Either she did not wish to speak to him, or she had gone away — his last call had been at one o'clock in the morning — and neither solution was particularly conducive to an easy mind.

As they swung into the avenue and drew up outside the broken gate of Whispering Beeches, Anthony could have sworn that he saw the green coupé disappearing up the road, and mentioned the fact to the superintendent. Budd smiled as he got laboriously down and entered the weed-grown drive.

'You've got green cars on the brain,' was his comment. 'I don't think you need worry about that coupé. I — if it was the same car, it's miles away by now.'

Anthony glanced at him sharply. He had a sudden feeling that the superintendent had ended his sentence differently to the way he had at first intended, but Budd was staring at the house ahead, his face expressionless. Even in the bright sunlight of that autumn morning it looked forbidding — a dark, gloomy pile of age-old red brick and grimy lichen-covered stone. The trees that grew around it were whispering mournfully as they shed their leaves in rustling cascades.

The big man went up the broken steps to the porch, taking a heavy bunch of keys from his pocket as he did so and, selecting one, inserted it in the lock. It turned easily without a sound, and Mr. Budd grunted.

'Recently oiled,' he muttered, and pushed the massive door inwards.

Even as it started to swing there came a scream from the drive behind them and, turning sharply, Anthony saw the figure of a woman running swiftly towards them.

'Come away!' she screamed breathlessly as she ran. 'Come away from that door.'

It was Mollie Trayne!

7

Mr. Jeffrey Tallent

The Rosebud looked round, his hand still on the knob, and the door open some two or three inches.

'Come away!' panted the girl. 'There is danger there — terrible danger!'

'What kind of danger?' asked Mr. Budd softly. To Anthony's astonishment he seemed not at all surprised at the sudden appearance of Mollie.

'I don't know,' she breathed. 'But it's death to anyone who opens that door.'

'Hm!' The stout superintendent rubbed his chin. 'Well, the door's got to be opened somehow.' He looked about him thoughtfully, and presently his eyes lighted on a long wooden prop, part of an ancient pergola, that lay amongst the rank grass. 'The very thing,' he murmured, and went over to it. Returning with the pole, he placed it on the steps, one end against the door.

'Keep out of the way,' he said, and Anthony drew the woman to one side. Mr. Budd crouched in the shelter of the steps and, grasping the end of the prop, pushed firmly. It swung open wide, and at the same instant from within the dark hall came a shattering explosion!

A cloud of acrid smoke rolled out of the entrance, and Anthony heard the angry drone of a score of bullets as they whizzed down the drive.

'That's that!' remarked Mr. Budd calmly, and waited. But after the one deafening report all was quiet, and presently the Rosebud, who remained by far the coolest of the trio, struggled to his feet and began to mount the short flight of moss-grown steps.

'For heaven's sake, be careful!' whispered Anthony huskily. 'There may still be danger. There must have been more than one person lurking in the hall, and — '

The big superintendent shook his head gently. 'I don't think there is any more danger,' he said quietly, 'and I shall be surprised if there is anyone inside the house at all.' He looked back at Mollie, who was clinging to Anthony's arm, her face white and strained and her whole body trembling. 'I'm right, aren't I, Miss Trayne?' he asked.

To the reporter's surprise the woman nodded. She was incapable of speech, for she was still breathing heavily from her recent exertion, but the quick movement of her head was sufficient answer.

Mr. Budd disappeared through the doorway into the dark interior beyond, and Anthony was racking his brains in a further futile attempt to solve the problem of Mollie's connection with this ill-omened house and the tragedy that seemed to envelop it, while he and the woman followed and passed into the gloomy hall. He felt her shiver slightly as they crossed the threshold, and guessed that she was recalling the last time they had stood together on that spot.

The Rosebud was standing by the foot of the big staircase, gazing thoughtfully down at a peculiar object that appeared to have been fixed to the banisters. As Anthony and the girl approached, he looked round and rubbed softly at his upper lip with a fat forefinger.

'Most ingenious,' he murmured gently. 'Very clever indeed.' He lowered his eyes once more to the object that had inspired this token of admiration and, following the direction of his gaze, Anthony saw in the dim light that filtered through the open front door a double-barrelled shotgun that had been lashed securely to the newel post, the muzzle pointing directly towards the entrance. He saw also the fine wire that was attached to the trigger and which ran through a tiny eyelet in the floor to a staple in the jamb, and from thence to a small hook screwed into the woodwork of the lower part of the door itself.

'Very clever indeed,' murmured the superintendent again. 'You see — ' He pointed to the wire. ' — the act of opening the front door pulled this wire taut and fired the gun — the wire being left sufficiently slack so as not to act until the door was pushed wide. A really brilliant idea, for it would be next to impossible for anybody to enter in the ordinary course of events without being riddled with bullets.'

Mollie surveyed the murder trap with horror-filled eyes. 'I — I was only just in time,' she muttered huskily.

'You were,' agreed Mr. Budd, looking deliberately and ponderously about him. 'Owing to my — er — rather generous proportions, I should undoubtedly have offered a very excellent target.'

'It was certainly lucky for us,' said Anthony, and then, turning to the woman curiously: 'But what were you doing here at all? How did you know about this gun arrangement?'

'The intuition of women is notorious,' remarked the Rosebud sententiously, before she had time to reply, 'and cannot be accounted for in any practical way. It is sufficient that Miss Trayne was the means of saving us from — to put it mildly — a very — er — unpleasant experience.'

Anthony stared at him in amazement not unmixed with a certain amount of annoyance. What was Budd getting at? As plainly as if he had put it in so many words, he was telling her not to answer his — Anthony's — question. Another thing that puzzled the reporter even more was that the superintendent had twice addressed her by name, and so far as Anthony knew he had never seen her before in his life! It was all very puzzling, and he began to feel that he had been swamped in a sea of mystery that had neither beginning nor end, and the very people from whom he might — with reason — expect candour and openness only made matters worse.

He opened his mouth to remonstrate on this state of affairs, but very wisely thought better of it, and remained silent. Later he would, perhaps, have an opportunity to question Mollie by herself, and learn something of the reason why she was so inextricably mixed up with the whole mysterious business.

Mr. Budd was engaged in peering up into the shadows of the staircase and was apparently oblivious of the thoughts to which his peculiarities had given rise in his friend's brain, for presently he turned with a genial smile and suggested that they might like to accompany him on a tour of the house.

'Not that I expect to find anything in particular,' he remarked, shrugging his broad shoulders. 'But curiosity always was a weakness of mine, and I'm curious to know several things.'

He paused for a moment, running his hand lightly up and down the flat oak rail of the banisters. 'For instance, I'm curious to know why there is so little dust on this staircase and such a lot everywhere else, and I'm curious to know why the hinges of that front door have been recently oiled, and why a man was murdered here two nights ago, and who it is who is in the habit of spending so much time in a house that has been shut up and empty for years, and why. And, above all, I'm curious to learn just why that gun was fixed to these stairs, and for whom it was intended.'

'It's easy enough to answer your last question,' said Anthony.

Mr. Budd looked at him as though he were gazing over the tops of an invisible pair of glasses — a disconcerting trick he possessed when someone had made a remark that afforded him amusement.

'You think so?' he asked gently.

'Don't you?' demanded the young reporter. 'Obviously it was intended for us. These people, whoever they are, must have got wind of the fact that you intended to come here to have a look round, and planted that gun in order to put you out of the running.'

'It sounds fine,' said the big superintendent, but he shook his head all the same. 'No, that gun wasn't put there for me — or you. It was put there — ' He broke off and, bending slightly forward, listened intently.

The click of the gate came distinctly to Anthony's ears, followed by the sound of heavy steps crunching on the gravel. Somebody was coming up the drive!

Moving with extraordinary agility for one of his enormous bulk, Mr. Budd slipped past Anthony and the woman, and took up his stand in the shadow thrown by the open front door.

The footsteps approached rapidly, stopped for a moment at the foot of the steps, and then began to ascend slowly.

Presently the figure of a man appeared silhouetted against the square of daylight — a short, rather wizened figure dressed in a tight-fitting black overcoat and carrying a neatly furled umbrella. As it came into view, the Rosebud stepped forward and greeted the newcomer. 'Good morning, Mr. Tallent,' he said pleasantly. 'I am rather surprised to see you here, but as you see, I have lost no time in making use of the keys which you so kindly placed at my disposal.'

The man in black gave a sharp, quick nod rather like an underfed bird pecking at a worm. 'I guessed it was you, Superintendent,' he said in a high reedy voice, 'when I saw that the front door was open — in fact, I hoped to find you here.'

As he came to a standstill on the top step, with the light full on him, Anthony was able to see him more clearly. He was an elderly man with a slither of grey side-whiskers and a long hatchet-shaped face, which a large and aggressive nose rendered the more hawk-like. His eyes were almost entirely concealed beneath bushy, overhanging brows, and his mouth was a mere slit, with thin, bloodless and tightly-compressed lips that he appeared to be constantly drawing inwards. Altogether Mr. Tallent possessed anything but a prepossessing personality, Anthony concluded; and his feelings on this point seemed to be shared in no small degree by Mollie, for he felt her fingers tighten on his arm and, looking down, surprised an expression that was akin to fear in her wide eyes.

'It is seldom that I find myself in this neighbourhood,' the thin voice went on. 'But as a matter of business brought me here this morning, and since I thought it was likely you might be somewhere on the — er — premises, I decided that I would call on the off-chance, and accompany you during your survey of the house.' The lawyer cleared his throat. 'It is nearly two years now since I was here,' he continued, 'er — that is personally. My managing clerk, of course — er — pays a periodical visit of inspection and — ' Mr. Tallent suddenly became aware of the presence of Anthony and the woman and broke off abruptly, peering at them short-sightedly.

'This is a friend of mine,' the Rosebud hastened to fill the rather sudden silence, and introduced Anthony and Mollie.

The lawyer bowed stiffly. 'You were the young man who discovered the — er — tragedy here, were you not?' he asked, and the reporter nodded. 'A dreadful occurrence,' said Mr. Tallent, dismally shaking his head, 'and absolutely ruinous to the value of the property. After the other affair it was impossible to let it, but I was hoping that time would erase that unpleasant memory. Now, however . . . ' He shook his head again and turned towards the superintendent. 'Am I too late?' he inquired. 'Have you already completed your inspection of the place?'

'No, we have only just got here,' answered the Rosebud.

'Then possibly I can be of assistance to you,' said Mr. Tallent, 'and also assure myself that the property is being kept in proper repair.' He crossed the threshold and looked about the dusty hall. As his roving eyes encountered the murder-machine fixed to the stairs, he started perceptibly. 'What — what is that?' he asked in a voice that was almost a croak.

The big superintendent regarded him with a fishy eye. 'That is what one might describe as a trap,' he replied, and proceeded to explain briefly the barrage that had greeted them when they had first arrived at the sinister house. Anthony noticed, however, that he omitted all reference to the part Mollie had played in that unpleasant episode.

Mr. Tallent's long, lean face went white; or, to be more accurate, it assumed a lighter shade of dusky grey as he listened in silence to Mr. Budd's graphic description. At the end he emitted a sharp, hissing breath as though he had been holding it in check during the superintendent's recital. 'Good heavens!' he exclaimed. 'What a dreadful thing! What a ghastly thing! Why, if I had arrived a few minutes earlier, I might easily have fallen a victim to this monstrous contraption.'

The Rosebud nodded. 'Quite easily,' he answered, and Anthony wondered whether he imagined the almost imperceptible stress he laid on the first word.

The lawyer stooped and examined the

gun, touching it gingerly with his gloved hand. 'I suppose there is no danger now?' he asked.

'Not the slightest,' replied the big man. 'It's as harmless as a boy's popgun.'

Mr. Tallent slowly straightened up. 'Have you any idea what can be at the bottom of all these — er — extraordinary occurrences?' he inquired. 'I should imagine there must be some — er — very good reason behind the recent events that have taken place in this house.'

'I'm sure there is a very good reason,' answered the superintendent heavily, 'and if I knew what it was, I should feel a great deal happier than I do at the moment.' He consulted a large gold watch, which he took from his pocket with the slow deliberation common to men of his bulk. 'I should like to get my examination of the premises over as soon as possible,' he continued. 'I have a rather important engagement at lunchtime, and — '

'Certainly, certainly,' interposed the lawyer hastily. 'I fear that I have unwittingly been the cause of delaying you; but naturally, since I am — er — the trustee of the property, I take a considerable interest in the place. You will begin, of course, with this floor?'

To Anthony's surprise, Mr. Budd shook his large head. 'I should prefer to start by inspecting the basement,' he murmured, 'and also any cellars there may be.'

'In that case I will remain here until you return,' remarked the lawyer with a mirthless smile. 'I am a martyr to rheumatism, and from what I can recall, the lower part of these premises is rather damp. You will find the way down through that door.' He pointed with a black-gloved hand towards a door under the big staircase. 'The key should be hanging on a nail beside it,' he added.

Mr. Budd walked over to the door, found the key and unlocked it.

'Perhaps — er — the young lady would prefer to remain up here?' suggested the lawyer. 'It is, no doubt, rather dirty and — '

'No — no, I'd like to go, too,' broke in Mollie quickly, and Anthony decided that for some reason of her own she was terrified at the idea of being left alone with this gaunt man in black.

Mr. Tallent gave an almost imperceptible shrug of his thin shoulders. 'Very well, then,' he remarked. Taking a handkerchief from his breast pocket, he spread it daintily on the lower stair and sat himself down. 'You will find me waiting you when you return.'

The Rosebud had already disappeared into the black depths beyond the narrow door. As Anthony and the woman gingerly made their way down the wooden stairway, they could hear him moving about below and caught a glimpse of light flashing along a broad stone-flagged passage.

'Why are you afraid of that skinny old devil?' asked Anthony in a whisper as they reached the bottom.

Mollie made no reply, and before he could repeat his question the big superintendent joined them, holding in his hand an electric torch. 'Somebody has been here, and recently,' he remarked in a low voice. 'Look at those tracks in the dust.'

He directed the light of the lamp on the floor, and Anthony saw a confused trail of footprints crossing and re-crossing the stone passage. Glancing aside, he saw something else and drew in his breath with a sharp hiss.

'What's that — over there by the wall?' he muttered huskily. Following the line of his pointing finger with the light, Mr. Budd uttered a quick exclamation and went over to the place.

Close up against the crumbling plaster was a dark patch, and it didn't need a second glance to assure him that it was dried blood!

8

The Thing in the Cellar

Stooping, he looked at the sinister stain more closely, and then felt it with his finger. 'That wasn't made so very long ago, I'll swear,' he remarked softly. 'Now, the question is — how did it get here, and whose blood is it?'

Mollie, who was peering over his shoulder, suddenly gave a little cry and pointed to a spot a few yards further along. 'There's another — there!' she said excitedly, and turning sharply the Rosebud flashed his light ahead. The girl had spoken the truth. Not quite so close to the wall and smaller than the first, but plainly visible, was a second blood mark.

'This is getting interestin',' murmured Mr. Budd as he moved over towards it.

'It looks to me as though somebody passed along here who was wounded,' commented Anthony. 'Though why they should have come here, heaven only knows.'

'And the person himself — if he knew anything about it, which I'm inclined to doubt,' said the superintendent cryptically, his eyes searching the stone flags that comprised the flooring. 'Look, there are several more there!'

They went forward and found a regular trail of blood spots that led them from the passage through a large bare room that had evidently been the kitchen, to a heavy door set in the brick wall of a little wash-house beyond. In front of this door they found the largest stain of all — a big irregular patch that had soaked into the dust and dirt that disuse and time had accumulated everywhere.

Mr. Budd paused and surveyed the door for a moment in silence. Then he raised his arm and attempted to turn the handle. But the door remained immovable.

'Humph!' he grunted disappointedly. 'Locked! Now I wonder if the key's anywhere about.'

They made a hasty search, but there

was no sign of a key; and although the superintendent tried every key he carried with him and even borrowed Anthony's bunch, none of them would fit.

'There's nothing for it but to break the door in,' he remarked after he had exhausted them all, 'for I don't intend to leave this place until I've seen what's on the other side.'

Handing Anthony the electric torch, he placed his broad shoulder against the woodwork and pressed with all his force. At first nothing happened except a faint creak; and then suddenly, with a sharp crack, the screws supporting the lock were torn out and the door swung inwards. Mr. Budd went with it and, unable to regain his balance, was precipitated down a flight of four steps that lay beyond. He landed on the hard floor and uttered an exclamation that was more forceful than polite.

'Are you hurt?' inquired Anthony anxiously, leaning through the open doorway of the cellar and flashing the torch into the gloom.

'Only my dignity,' grunted Mr. Budd,

scrambling to his feet. 'Give me that light.' He stretched out his hand and took the torch from Anthony's grasp, sweeping it round him.

The white beam, cutting through the darkness, revealed a fairly large apartment of white-washed brick, grimy and festooned with cobwebs. The low roof was raftered obviously with the beams that supported the floor above.

The place was littered with mouldering straw and pieces of rotting wood and smelt horribly earthy and damp, reminding the superintendent of a tomb. It was apparently the place in which the previous tenants of Whispering Beeches had stored their coal, for at the far end he made out dimly a dark heap that glinted in the ray from his torch.

There seemed nothing at all to reward him for his trouble in getting in and, having taken a cursory glance round, he was in the act of turning to go back to Anthony and the woman when something nearly hidden under a heap of straw attracted his attention. It looked like the corner of a leather case of some description, and he went over to satisfy his curiosity, parting the straw to get a better view. Anthony heard his suppressed cry and called to him sharply.

'Come here for a moment will you?' said Mr. Budd, and there was the faintest trace of a quiver in his voice. 'No, don't bring Miss Trayne with you. Let her stay where she is.'

Anthony gave Mollie's arm a reassuring squeeze and, leaving her outside, entered the cellar. The Rosebud was stooping down in one corner and as the young reporter stumbled to his side, he looked up quickly. 'See that?' he whispered, pointing to a figure that lay motionless amid a heap of straw. 'That's where the blood came from!'

Anthony looked and went white and sick, for he was staring into the dead face of Louis Savini!

'Good heavens!' he muttered. 'How horrible!'

Mr. Budd nodded, and straightened his bulky form. 'The body was evidently brought here during the time you were unconscious.' He spoke rapidly in a low tone. 'And I shall have something to say to Wiles for not finding it when he came and searched the house. Obviously he never came down here at all, otherwise he couldn't have failed to see those bloodstains.'

'But what was the object?' inquired Anthony. 'Why did they go to the trouble of bringing the — the — ' He paused. 'That — down here?'

'For the simple reason that if you had recovered consciousness and found the actual body in the room with you,' answered the superintendent, 'you would in all probability have called the police then and there. Not finding it, they hoped that after reading that note you would decide to say nothing more about the affair. The last thing they wanted was any form of publicity attaching to this house.' He looked down once more at the still and silent form of the dead man. 'I'll call in at the nearest police station and send an ambulance to collect this poor chap's remains. In the meantime, I think we'd better keep this discovery to ourselves.'

Anthony nodded dazedly. His brain was

reeling with an effort to find some clear and convincing reason for the queer whirl of apparently disconnected incidents into which accident and his own curiosity had plunged him. Of only one thing was he certain, and that was that the Rosebud knew or guessed a great deal more about the whole matter than he said — and so also did Mollie. That to Anthony was the biggest mystery of the lot, and he determined at the first opportunity to have a long talk to the woman and try if possible to get her to confide in him.

As they left the cellar and emerged once more into the cold and dusty scullery, Mollie came forward and laid her hand on Mr. Budd's arm.

'What did you find?' she asked eagerly, her large blue eyes searching his face inquiringly.

'Quite a lot of dust,' replied the Rosebud humorously, brushing himself down.

'But that wasn't all,' Mollie insisted. 'What did you call Tony for?'

'To kill a spider,' explained the superintendent carefully. 'I have an ingrained horror of spiders.'

The girl gave an impatient exclamation. 'Why won't you tell me?' she demanded angrily. 'You've found something in there — something important, and I want to know what it was.'

'I found — ' began Mr. Budd slowly, and stopped. From somewhere above them came the sound of a heavy thud — the closing of a door.

'What was that?' asked Anthony with a start, his nerves on edge.

'It sounded like the front door being slammed,' answered the superintendent. 'Perhaps old Tallent has got tired of waiting.'

'Surely he'd have called down and said he was going,' said Anthony, and Mr. Budd shrugged his shoulders.

'There's no knowing what he'd do,' he replied. 'He's an eccentric old chap. Perhaps he only shut the door because he was feeling cold. However, we'll go up and see.'

He led the way back through the kitchen and along the stone passage. Mollie lingered behind, her arm linked in Anthony's. 'Tell me what you found in that cellar,' she whispered softly.

'Why are you so anxious to know?' he countered in the same tone.

'Because I'm curious,' she answered.

'I'm curious about a lot of things concerning you,' said Anthony, 'but you won't tell me.'

'Only because I can't,' she said. 'Honestly I can't, Tony, or I would.'

'Is that why you've been avoiding me lately?' he asked as they followed Mr. Budd up the stairs to the hall.

'Yes, partly,' she replied candidly. 'I knew you'd ask me hundreds of questions that I couldn't answer — and besides, I've been very busy.'

'Doing what?' he demanded quickly.

'Oh, all sorts of things,' she said evasively. 'Now what was it you — '

The Rosebud's voice broke in upon her question, booming and echoing in the stillness of the vast hall. 'There's certainly nobody here,' he remarked. 'So unless he's in some other part of the house he must have gone. Mr. Tallent!' He raised his voice, calling loudly. 'Mr. Tallent! Mr. Tallent!'

But there was no reply. Only the hollow echoes of the name went rolling round the upper floors and were repeated faintly and mockingly.

'He's gone, or else he's taking a walk round the grounds,' said Mr. Budd. 'Well, in either case we can't waste any more time. We'll just have a quick look over the house and then go.' He glanced at Anthony. 'Which is the room where you found Savini?' he asked.

Anthony pointed to the door on the right of the hall. 'In there,' he replied, and the superintendent walked over to it, grasped the handle, and flung the door open.

'Come and show me — ' he began, and then broke off sharply, standing rigid and motionless on the threshold of the room, his eyes staring and his jaw dropped.

Anthony reached his side and looked in. The next moment he gave a cry in which horror and amazement were curiously mingled.

'Really, this is getting a trifle monotonous,' remarked Mr. Budd wearily, stepping into the room.

9

The Disappearance of Anthony

Anthony Gale banged out the last word on his battered typewriter, collected the half-dozen sheets of neat typescript that strewed his writing table and, adding the one he had just finished working on, sat back in his chair and read through the result of his labours.

A satisfied smile played round his lips as he reached the end and clipped the sheets neatly together, for he had been typing an account of the latest developments in the Sinister House Mystery, as Mr. Downer had titled it; and for sheer sensationalism, Anthony concluded, it was calculated to please the heart of even that difficult and news-hardened man.

He folded the sheets, slipped them into an envelope, and laid them aside ready for the special messenger who was calling for them at nine o'clock to take them to the offices of the *Courier* for delivery into the tender keeping of the news-editor.

Stretching himself, Anthony rose and lighting a cigarette, crossed over to the comfortable chair beside the glowing gas fire. The little clock that ticked cheerfully on the mantelpiece informed him that it was barely half-past seven, so he had over an hour to idle away before the arrival of the Rosebud, who had promised to drop in and see him at eight-thirty.

Settling himself comfortably in the deep chair, Anthony allowed his mind to wander over the startling events of the day. After the discovery of the murdered lawyer on the exact spot where Savini had met his death, the stout superintendent had conducted a careful search of the entire house, but the result had proved disappointing.

There was little of interest, and nothing at all that shed any light upon the tragic happenings that had taken place within those grim and gloomy walls. Most of the rooms contained the original furniture, swathed in dustsheets that had been in use during Dr. Shard's residence, and the library and laboratory were practically intact, though everything was covered with a thick coating of dust.

Although they found no tangible clue to the meaning of the mystery that seemed to have its core in that weird and ill-omened mansion, there was plenty of evidence that others besides themselves had visited Whispering Beeches whilst it was unoccupied, for there were footmarks everywhere — footmarks of more than one person — and every drawer and cupboard in the place had been opened and ransacked. Even the books on the long shelves in the library had been moved from their resting places and tumbled in disorderly heaps on the floor, and in several places the rotting panelling had been torn bodily from the walls. Without a shadow of a doubt the house had been subjected to a rigorous search. But for what?

Anthony had put this very question to the stout Mr. Budd just before he had taken leave of that gentleman at the gate, after the arrival of the local inspector, but the superintendent had apparently grown suddenly deaf. That Budd had more than a vague idea as to the meaning of it all, Anthony felt certain, and he made up his mind to tackle him about his knowledge that evening.

His thoughts switched to Mollie. He had tried to persuade the woman to allow him to take her for a belated lunch, but she had pleaded a headache, and had even refused his company back to her flat. She had promised, however, to meet him for tea at Pelli's on the following afternoon, which had to some extent mitigated her rather abrupt departure.

Anthony had got one item of news which he thought would be of interest to Mr. Budd. The green car with the silver Statue of Liberty had passed his cottage while he was in the act of putting his key in the lock, and this time he had managed to catch a glimpse of the occupants.

The driver he failed to recognize, but the slim figure seated by his side was unmistakable, for he had got a full view of her profile. What Mollie had been doing in the car which appeared to spend its time trailing him about had occupied

Anthony's thoughts for most of the afternoon, but he had failed to reach any satisfactory conclusion, and had at last given it up in despair.

That the woman was a crook he steadfastly refused to believe, and yet she had been friendly with Savini; had obviously known about the presence of the murder-trap set for someone in the sinister house, and was on intimate terms apparently with the owner of the green car.

It was true he knew very little about her. His first meeting with her six months previously had been the result of a request to pass the sugar in a popular teashop. From this small beginning had developed a friendship which had rapidly ripened into something more — a sort of vague understanding between them, which had been very pleasant until Savini had stepped in and spoiled it all.

Anthony sat on, letting his thoughts wander where they would, until a sharp rat-tat on the front door put an end to his reverie.

Mr. Budd stood on the step, buttoned

up to the chin in a voluminous overcoat, his good-natured face one large expansive smile. 'I've been tremendously busy,' he announced cheerfully, after he had divested himself of his enormous outer garment and carefully lowered his huge bulk into the largest of Anthony's chairs.

'That's a change,' said the reporter. 'I shall be interested to hear what you've been doing.'

'You will, my boy,' answered Mr. Budd, holding the drink Anthony had poured out for him in a chubby hand and regarding it with a loving eye. 'I've discovered something this afternoon which I have suspected for a long time, but have never been lucky enough to prove.'

'Well, what is it?' demanded Anthony impatiently.

The Rosebud looked at him over invisible glasses. 'I have discovered that Mr. Tallent was a crook,' he said impressively. He took a long drink and nodded. 'A crook!' he repeated. 'And not only a crook, but a murderer!'

'Good heavens!' exclaimed the startled reporter. 'You don't mean that he

— Savini — ' He broke off incoherently.

'No, no,' replied The Rosebud. 'If you mean did he kill Savini. I am referring to a gentleman of the name of Selton, who was discovered at six o'clock this evening in the hall of an empty house in Lambeth, shot in the back.'

Anthony stared at him and passed a hand wearily across his forehead.

'I'm all mixed up,' he said dazedly. 'Who's Selton, anyway, and what's he got to do with it all?'

'I will explain,' said Mr. Budd, emptying his glass and setting it down in the fender.

'It would be just as well,' said Anthony sarcastically. 'And while you're about it there are several other questions I'd like you to answer as well.'

' 'Ask and ye shall receive,' ' quoted The Rosebud. 'I'm in a communicative mood this evening.'

'Well, that's something to be thankful for, anyway,' said the reporter fervently. 'Carry on — spill your end of it.'

Mr. Budd reached over to the table for a cigarette and lighted it carefully.

'As I told you,' he began, studying the glowing end intently, 'we have for a long time had our suspicions regarding Tallent. Several odd rumours have reached our ears. Nothing very tangible, but sufficient to lead us to suppose that under the cloak of his legal business he was carrying on the illicit but profitable one of a fence.'

'A what?' exclaimed the astonished Anthony.

'A receiver of stolen property,' explained Mr. Budd, inhaling a deep breath of smoke.

'I know what you mean,' said the reporter impatiently. 'But a fence — good lor'!'

'It does sound astonishing, doesn't it?' admitted the superintendent. 'But it's a fact all the same. We have been practically sure of it for months, but we've never been able to collect a single atom of evidence against him — until today.' He paused and cleared his throat. 'Tallent's tragic death at Whispering Beeches gave us — or rather me — the opportunity of examining his private papers, and if there was a lack of evidence before there is certainly sufficient now. What a pity — '

He shook his head sadly. ' — that it is too late to act upon!'

'But what about this fellow Selton, or whatever his name is?' asked Anthony. 'How does he come into it?'

'He doesn't come into it,' replied the Rosebud with a sigh. 'He's gone out of it. He went out of it, according to the divisional surgeon, thirty-six hours ago.' He took a long pull at his cigarette, slowly exhaled a cloud of smoke and continued. 'Among the various incriminating documents which we found in Tallent's private safe was a book which set down clearly the many transactions in which he had been involved, and also the names of the crooks with whom he had done business — an interestin' collection. There was mention, too, of an address in Lambeth at which apparently Tallent was in the habit of meeting his criminal associates. I lost no time in visiting the place, and found not only a considerable amount of further evidence against him, but at the foot of the stairs the dead body of a well-known little sneak-thief — Selton by name. He had been shot twice in the back and it was obviously a case of murder. The hand that struck down Tallent in that room at Whispering Beeches saved the hangman a job.'

Anthony leant against the edge of the writing-table and thrust his hands into his pockets.

'What connection is there between all this and the other business?' he demanded. 'What had Tallent got to do with that? You say he didn't kill Savini, so — '

Mr. Budd waved a fat hand protestingly. 'You go too fast,' he objected. 'The connection between the late lamented Mr. Tallent and the strange occurrences at Sinister House is slightly involved — so involved that I'm not even sure if my theory is the right one or not.'

'What is your theory?' asked the reporter quickly.

The Rosebud carefully crushed out the stub of his cigarette in the ash-tray. 'That would entail rather a long explanation,' he began, 'and I don't know whether I should be justified yet in — '

'Look here,' broke in Anthony impatiently, 'stop beating about the bush and answer me a plain question. Do you know what is at the bottom of these murders and the gun incident and all the rest of it?'

Mr. Budd considered once more, regarding his friend over the top of his invisible glasses. 'I have a very good idea,' he replied after a slight pause. 'Yes, I have a very good idea.'

'Then for heaven's sake, let's hear it!' snapped the reporter.

'Unless I'm entirely wrong,' said the Rosebud, 'the whole thing hinges on the murder of Dr. Shard and the fact that he was engaged in trying to find a cure for cancer at the time of his death.'

'What in the world has a cure for cancer got to do with it?' interrupted the reporter in amazement.

'Everything,' said Mr. Budd decisively. 'It is the motive behind the entire affair. It is the reason for Savini's murder. It was the reason for Dr. Shard's death originally, and it is the reason why the enterprising career of Mr. Tallent was cut off in its prime — a cure for cancer and a certain little key that is at the moment safely deposited in your bank.'

'Do you think if you tried very hard,' said Anthony wearily, 'you could stop emulating the detective of fiction and tell me what you're driving at without talking in riddles?'

'I'm driving at this,' replied the Rosebud. 'Radium!'

'Eh?'

'Radium,' repeated the superintendent.

'What the dickens do you mean by radium?' cried the exasperated Anthony.

'A rather rare substance obtained from pitchblende — ' began Mr. Budd gently.

'I know what it is,' shouted the reporter. 'You needn't air your profound knowledge of chemistry.'

'There you are, you see,' objected the Rosebud in an injured voice. 'When I do speak plainly, you're not satisfied.'

'Good heavens!' Anthony rubbed the back of his neck in despair. 'Do you fondly imagine that you're speaking plainly when you keep on repeating the word like a — like a parrot?'

'If you didn't keep on interrupting me,' said Mr. Budd, the chair creaking in protest as he crossed a massive leg, 'I would try to make things clear to your dull intellect. That key which you picked up on the night Savini met his death — by the way, I should like you to let me have it first thing in the morning — is the — ' He stopped abruptly as there came a loud, peremptory knock on the front door.

'That's my messenger from the *Courier* offices,' said Anthony, glancing at the clock. 'He's early — it's only ten to nine.' He picked up the envelope from the writing-table. 'I won't be a minute,' he flung back over his shoulder and left the room.

The Rosebud heard him hurry along the tiny hall and open the front door, heard the faint murmur of a man's voice, then the slam of the door, followed by the sound of receding footsteps outside. Reaching out his hand he helped himself to a fresh cigarette and lighted it, flicking the used match neatly into Anthony's big ashtray.

A moment passed, but the reporter did not come back. Wondering what he was doing, Mr. Budd called to him. There was no reply. The superintendent called again louder, but nothing but silence answered him.

With a sudden feeling of uneasiness he hoisted himself out of the chair and went out into the darkened hall. The light from the open door of the room he had just left was sufficient to show him that the hall was empty. Opening the front door, he looked out into the night. It was pitch dark, and a slight drizzle of rain had begun to fall, but there was no sign of Anthony. Mr. Budd walked down the little path and gazed up the deserted road right and left. The red tail-light of a car was vanishing in the distance — a tiny spark that disappeared even as he watched it — but there was no other human life stirring.

Now thoroughly alarmed, the Rosebud retraced his steps and made a hurried search of the cottage. Except for himself, it was empty. Anthony had walked out of his study and vanished — as completely as though a giant hand had reached out of the blackness of the night and snatched him from the world!

10

The Man with the Ivory Hands

Anthony stirred uneasily, conscious of an unaccustomed restriction to his limbs and a dull throbbing in his head. Opening his eyes, he stared up at a low ceiling, and tried unsuccessfully at first to force his still-dazed brain into some semblance of normal action. Desperately he tried to recall what had happened.

He remembered leaving the Rosebud in the study at his cottage and going out into the hall to open the door to the messenger from the *Courier*; remembered facing a strange man on the step who had inquired his name in a low voice; and then something had sprayed in his face. From that time until now had been a blank, or almost a blank. He had been dimly aware, as in a vague dream, of being caught as he fell forward in a pair of strong arms and carried somewhere, and later of the noise of an engine at close quarters. After that complete unconsciousness had descended upon him, broken only by one faint impression of rain falling on his face.

As the mists gradually rolled away from his senses, Anthony began to feel an intense curiosity concerning his immediate surroundings, and raising his aching head with difficulty looked about him.

He was lying on a straw mattress in a long, narrow, low-roofed apartment that appeared to be some sort of cellar, or at any rate situated underground, for a musty, damp odour percolated to his nostrils and the bare brick walls glistened with drops of water. Near at hand was a large packing case, and on this stood an oil storm-lantern which supplied the sole means of illumination to this depressing chamber.

Opposite to where he lay, almost invisible in the shadows that cloaked that end of the room, was a heavy door. There was nothing else in the place, no other scrap of furniture beyond the mattress and the packing case, if they could be dignified by such a name. Having seen all there was to see, Anthony turned his attention to the bonds that secured his wrists and ankles. A few seconds' experiment convinced him that they had been tied by an expert, for though he tried his utmost, the thin cords refused to yield a fraction of an inch.

He lay back again on the hard mattress and thought over his position. It was anything but a pleasant one, for he had no delusions as to who had been responsible for this audacious abduction or the reason he had been brought to this unsavoury place, wherever it was. Without a doubt it was the work of the people at whose hands Savini and Tallent had met their deaths. He wondered how long he had been unconscious, but there was no means of telling. It was impossible to see his wristwatch, for his hands had been tied behind his back.

It seemed to Anthony that an age passed before the faint sound of a shuffling footstep broke the silence. It came from the direction of the door, and was followed almost at once by the rasping of a key in the lock. As Anthony stared across at it, the door began to open slowly, and there emerged out of the shadows the figure of a man. He was short and squat and dressed in a long black coat that reached almost to his heels. His face was entirely concealed beneath a black silk handkerchief that he wore around his head, and in which two slits had been cut for his eyes.

Moving in the circle of light cast by the lantern, with a curious shuffling gait as though his knees were perpetually bent, he stood regarding the prostrate figure of the young reporter in silence. Watching the sinister figure, Anthony felt a little icy shiver trickle up his spine and the cause was neither the masked face, nor the evil glittering eyes that stared unblinkingly from the holes in the silk. It was the hands held half-clenched in front of him. For they were long and talon-like, of the colour of old ivory, and so thin that the bones showed clearly. The hands of the man he had fought with in that empty room at Whispering Beeches on the night Louis Savini had been done to death!

'We meet again, Mr. Gale.' The voice was gentle, almost musical, but with a sibilant hissing timbre that sounded indescribably menacing.

Anthony returned the other's steady gaze without flinching, but remained silent.

'I regret that I have been forced to put you to this inconvenience,' went on the masked man, loosely clasping his claw-like hands in front of him, 'but unfortunately there was no other way. There is a slight service which it is in your power to render me, and which I am sure — ' He laid a meaning stress on the last word. ' — you will not refuse.'

'You seem to take a lot for granted.' Anthony raised his eyebrows slightly.

The man in black inclined his head. 'Merely because,' he said slowly, 'I have a profound knowledge of human nature — and its weaknesses.'

The words were ordinary and quietly spoken, almost whispered, and yet they sent an involuntary shiver through Anthony as he heard them. There was a finality — an underlying threat in the tone of the voice that made his flesh creep. This shapeless figure in its long black coat, with those horrible ivory hands, radiated an almost palpable atmosphere of evil and something more — a relentless force of will that dominated. This creature would go to any lengths of devilry to attain his ends.

'What is it you want me to do?' asked Anthony after a slight pause, though he already guessed what the reply would be.

'A mere trifle,' was the answer. 'You have — or rather, you had — in your possession a leather wallet which you picked up in the hall at Whispering Beeches. If my information is correct, you have since deposited it with your bankers. All that I require you to do is write a letter to your bank manager, instructing him to hand that wallet over to the bearer of the note.'

'Is that all?' inquired Anthony calmly.

'That is all,' said the man in black.

'And after I've written this letter — what happens then?' continued the reporter in the same level voice.

'You will remain here for thirty-six hours,' replied the other, 'at the expiration of which time I will undertake to have you released.'

'I see,' said Anthony.

'You are prepared to do this?' There was a slight upward cadence in the tone and the only outward sign of excitement visible.

'No, I'll see you in hell first,' said Anthony without heat.

The man in black exhaled a sibilant breath, and his eyes glittered through the slits in the silk handkerchief. 'I was hoping,' he grated, failing to keep the fury out of his voice, 'that you were going to be sensible.'

'I think I am being very sensible,' retorted Anthony.

'No doubt,' sneered the other harshly, his hands so tightly clasped that the knuckles stood out white against the yellow skin. 'However I believe that I shall be able to persuade you to do what I ask.'

'There's nothing like being an optimist,' said the reporter. 'But if you think you are going to get hold of that wallet, you've made a big mistake. It'll remain where it is until I go and fetch it myself.'

The masked man shook his head. 'I fear that you are labouring under a delusion,' he hissed softly. 'I assure you that I have several means at my command to force you to do what I desire.' He paused and leaned slightly forward. 'Several years ago,' he continued, speaking slowly and deliberately, so that every word received its full value, 'I lived for some time in China — a marvellous country, Mr. Gale, and a marvellous race. They have evolved methods for persuading obstinate people to become . . . shall we say tractable? — that are extraordinarily ingenious and — er — painful.'

Anthony compressed his lips. There was no mistaking the meaning that lay behind the cold ferocity of that emotionless voice.

'If you continue in your pig-headed refusal to write that necessary letter to your bank,' went on the man in black, 'I am afraid that I shall be compelled to initiate you into the more refined — er — methods invented by the Chinese.' He gave a little cackling laugh. 'Perhaps you may have heard of the wire jacket!'

The blood receded from Anthony's face, leaving it white and strained. He had heard of the wire jacket — that most diabolical of all the diabolical instruments invented for the torture of man by man.

'I see that you are well acquainted with the little — er — toy to which I have referred,' chuckled the other. 'Well that makes it easier for you to understand what will inevitably be the result if you don't reconsider your decision.'

The momentary feeling of cold fear left Anthony, and was succeeded by a flaming wave of rage against this sneering, chuckling devil before him that engulfed his senses in a red mist. 'You beastly mass of corrupt humanity,' he burst out hoarsely. 'You can try all the damned tortures that you've picked up during your loathsome existence, but if you chop me into little pieces I won't write that letter!'

The black-garbed figure drew in his breath with a sharp whistling sound and took a step forward. For a moment Anthony thought he was going to strike him, but with a supreme effort he mastered the rage that was consuming him and bending down, stared the reporter full in the face. 'We shall see,' he said between his teeth, and the words came like the hiss of a venomous snake. 'I shall be interested to know whether, after the little demonstration I have in store for you, you will continue to remain in the same mind as you are at present.'

Straightening up, he turned abruptly away and shuffled over to the door. Opening it, he called softly into the blackness beyond. There was a long silence and then two other figures entered the cellar-like chamber. The first was a tall, thin man enveloped in a soiled mackintosh and wearing a black handkerchief about his face similar to that worn by the man with the ivory hands. He was gripping the wrists of the second figure, whose wide horror-filled eyes stared wildly about the dimly lit chamber as she was dragged in roughly through the narrow doorway.

Anthony's heart almost stopped beating, and his throat went suddenly dry and hard as he recognized the white-faced woman. So Mollie Trayne was to be the means by which he was to be forced to sign that letter.

11

The Wire Mask

The short, squat figure in the black coat gave a low, malignant chuckle as he saw the expression on Anthony's face. 'Quite an unexpected development, eh, Mr. Gale?' he sneered. 'And calculated rather to upset your heroic theories.'

Anthony was silent, his eyes fixed on the slim figure of Mollie. She was in evening dress and her bare white arms and shoulders gleamed in the dim light of the lantern. A gag had been tied about her mouth, but the expression in her eyes as they met Anthony's spoke volumes. Amazement, horror and despair — a whole gamut of varying emotions changed swiftly in those blue depths. But there was not a trace of fear. She was aware of her danger but still retained her nerve, and Anthony felt a little thrill of pride as he watched her calm, almost contemptuous bearing.

The masked man began speaking again softly and deliberately, obviously enjoying the situation. 'Before proceeding any further,' he said, shuffling to the centre of the low room, and taking up a position so that he stood between Anthony and the girl, 'I will give you a last chance to behave sensibly. Are you prepared to sign a letter on the lines that I have already suggested?'

Anthony hesitated. He guessed the reason for Mollie's presence, and the knowledge filled his soul with a cold dread. Anything was better than that she should be harmed. She evidently realized the struggle that was taking place within him, for he saw her give an almost imperceptible shake of her head. The action decided him. After all, if he could only gain time, something might happen. Budd would have discovered his absence almost at once, and would immediately set the complicated machinery of Scotland Yard in motion. There was time enough to give in to this devil's demands at the last moment when every hope had gone.

'I will sign nothing,' said Anthony shortly.

The other nodded his head slowly, and made a gesture to the man who was standing by Mollie's side. Leaving the woman, he went out, carefully shutting the door behind him.

'It is a great pity,' said the man in black when he had gone, 'for the subsequent proceedings will be entirely your own fault.' He paused and looked from Anthony to the girl and back again. 'I think we were discussing the Chinese methods for breaking down the resistance of unruly prisoners,' he continued quietly, and his tone was almost conversational. 'And if I remember rightly, I mentioned the wire jacket. It is a cleverly constructed — er — little arrangement consisting of a cage of wire netting which is fastened about the upper part of the human body and screwed tight until the flesh protrudes in knobs through the mesh. The operator is armed with a sharp knife, and — no doubt your imagination can picture the result! I may add, however, that no one yet has succeeded in lasting out the full operation!'

He stopped, enjoying the look of horror

and disgust that had crossed Anthony's face.

'I do not, however, intend to use that excellent arrangement in the present circumstances, so I have evolved, using the idea of the wire jacket as a working basis, a little instrument which I flatter myself to be particularly ingenious. Our friend has gone to fetch it and when he returns I shall have great pleasure in giving you a practical demonstration.'

In spite of Mollie's self-control, Anthony saw for the first time a glint of fear creep into her eyes, and for a second she swayed slightly. She recovered herself almost at once, but the action had been sufficient to fill him with an almost overmastering rage against the cool, inhuman fiend who was speaking so easily and callously of unnameable horrors.

The man in black must have seen the hot flush that mounted to the reporter's face, for he gave one of his little cackling laughs and leaned forward. 'Even now,' he said, 'it is not too late for you to avoid all — er — unpleasantness. Just a stroke of the pen at the foot of a letter that is already typed in preparation for your signature, and — you need worry no more.'

'You're wasting your breath, you nasty little maggot!' replied Anthony, though his heart was beating thunderously and there was a horrible sick sensation in the pit of his stomach.

The masked man shrugged his hunched shoulders. 'Then Miss Trayne has only you to thank for any — er — painful experience to which she may be subjected,' he said harshly, and turned as the door opened and the other man entered.

He carried a large black box which he set down on the stone floor without speaking. The man with the ivory hands bent over it and raised the lid with a curious eagerness that Anthony found particularly revolting. Drawing out a strangely shaped object of wire, he held it out in the light of the lantern and turned his head to face the reporter,

'I've no doubt,' he said sneeringly, 'that you are consumed with curiosity. Therefore I will be as brief as possible. This mask which I have in my hand is my own improvement on the wire jacket. Its use I am about to show you.'

He shuffled over to Mollie and with a quick movement slipped the thing over her head. It covered her face and neck with a network of small-meshed wire netting, and rather resembled the masks used for fencing, save that it fitted more closely.

'Keep still!' he rasped, as the terrified girl made a movement backwards. 'It will not hurt you — yet.'

He adjusted a screw at the back of the mask and then shuffled back to the box, from which stretched two thin wires up to the thing that enclosed the girl's face.

'Before going any further,' said the man in black with a chuckle, 'I had better explain the principle on which my little invention works. In this box is a powerful battery, generating sufficient current to turn the wires of that mask round Miss Trayne's head white hot! It takes slightly over five minutes for them to reach the maximum temperature, but I can assure you that even at red heat the result is most — fascinating!'

A little strangled cry broke from Mollie's lips, and swaying, she would have fallen if the other man hadn't caught her in his arms. 'I think she's fainted, guv'nor,' he muttered in a deep voice as he supported her slim, drooping form.

The man in black uttered a snarl of annoyance. 'Never mind,' he rasped. 'Prop her up against the wall. She'll soon come to when I switch on the current — and she'll wish she hadn't!'

'You fiend!' burst out Anthony through lips that were white and bloodless. 'You can't do it!'

'Can't I?' hissed the other, stretching out one of those horrible hands to the box. 'I hate spoiling anything so beautiful, but you leave me no alternative.' His fingers groped inside the lid.

'Stop!' cried Anthony hoarsely, the per-spiration standing out in little beads on his forehead. 'Stop, I'll sign that letter!'

The masked man withdrew his hand and slowly straightened up. 'I thought you would,' he said with a note of triumph in his voice. 'Here!' He beckoned to the second man, who was standing beside the limp figure of Mollie. 'Leave the girl and come and untie his wrists.'

He drew an automatic from the pocket of his coat and covered Anthony. 'A little precaution in case you should feel tempted to do anything rash,' he sneered.

It took some time to loosen the cords about the reporter's wrists, for his struggles had tightened the knots; but it was done at last, and Anthony moved his cramped fingers about to restore the circulation.

'Here you are!' rasped the man in black, and thrust a paper in front of him.

'Before I sign this,' said Anthony, 'I want to know what's going to happen to Miss Trayne.'

'She will be left here with you and released — after my messenger has returned safely from the bank,' was the reply. 'So be very careful that your signature is not likely to evoke comment, for in that case — ' He left the sentence unfinished, but the threat was unmistakable.

With a shrug of his shoulders, Anthony took the pen that the second man held out to him. 'All right,' he said coolly, 'you win.' Laying the paper on the stone floor, he leaned over the side of the mattress and signed his name. 'There you are!' he grunted, and flung down the pen.

With an exultant laugh the man in black reached out a talon-like hand and picked up the letter. 'Bind his hands again,' he ordered sharply, and in silence he was obeyed. 'And the woman's ankles too, but take off the wire mask,' he added, and again the order was carried out. As soon as it was done the other man went out, leaving the door open.

'And now I will wish you a long farewell, Mr. Gale.' The masked man folded the letter and put it in his pocket, shuffling towards the door. 'I might as well tell you now,' he went on, pausing on the threshold, 'that I have no intention of coming back to release you. I warned you once to keep out of my affairs — you foolishly ignored that warning. This time I shall take steps to make it impossible for you to — er — bother me again.'

He went out, closing and locking the door, and Anthony heard his shuffling steps die away to silence. He looked over at Mollie. She was still seated, half-leaning against the wall, her head dropping forward on her breast. Anthony uttered a curse beneath his breath. He might have known that foul creature would never have let them go — had never had any intention of letting them go. He was racking his brains for a means of escape when a sudden sound made him raise his eyes quickly — a gurgling, splashing sound that was rapidly growing louder! Over in the shadows a steady stream of water was falling — pouring out from an orifice in one of the walls! Even as he looked it increased in volume, throwing up a cloud of spray as it struck the stone floor of the cellar.

Anthony writhed and twisted in a vain endeavour to free himself from his bonds. Already the water was creeping in an uneven stream over the floor and, at the rate it was entering, could scarcely take longer than half an hour at the most to engulf them! Helpless and panting from his futile exertions, Anthony lay back, watching the glittering cascade, and waited — for death!

12

Night Shadows

Night had come, and with it a fitful breeze that moaned through the beeches surrounding Sinister House, bending their skeleton heads so that they appeared to stoop and whisper to each other, and then draw angrily back as though annoyed at something they had heard.

Every now and again a pale moon gleamed momentarily from behind the wrack of leaden-hued clouds that were being driven mercilessly across the sky, and its white rays, touching for a second the twisted chimneys and gables of the gloomy pile, edged them with silver, so that from the roadway the place presented the appearance of a ghostly castle lifted bodily out of some ancient German legend.

Not that there was anyone about to see, for midnight had long since struck, and during those brief intervals when the moon peered down it shone blearily upon a sleeping world. And yet not altogether, for amid the tangle of rank grass and weeds and overgrown bushes that formed the grounds of Whispering Beeches something stirred — a vague shadow flitted out of the darkness and moved swiftly and noiselessly from tree to tree. Presently under the frowning wall of the house itself, it was joined by a second phantom shape that seemed to material-ize suddenly from the surrounding gloom, and human whisperings floated up to blend with the voices of the trees.

A drizzle of fine rain had begun to fall, and after a moment's conversation the two black-garbed figures drew their coats closer about them and made their way stealthily towards the steps leading up to the front entrance. There was the click of metal against metal, and silently the big heavy door opened, the shadows melted into the yawning chasm of blackness beyond, and the door closed again, leaving a stillness more profound because of that momentary evidence of life, and broken only by the gentle patter of the rain and the intermittent sighing of the wind.

Inside the large, dusty hall, the two who had entered stood listening intently, and so dark was it that though they were but a few inches apart neither could see the other. Suddenly a dazzling beam of white light shone out and focused on the staircase as the shorter of the twain produced an electric torch, and the reflected rays showed clearly the ivory hand and claw-like fingers that encircled the smooth barrel.

'The only danger was that the police might have had the place guarded after I settled my little score with Tallent.' The sibilant whisper sounded loud in that deathlike silence, though the words were uttered almost inaudibly. 'Still, I had a good look round earlier this evening, and again just before meeting you, and there was no sign of anybody.'

'So did I,' said the other and taller man. 'There's nobody here — the place is deserted.' He looked about him through the slits in the mask he wore and shivered. 'All the same, I shall be glad when we have finished what we came for, and get away. The house gives me the creeps.'

His companion gave a low, cackling chuckle. 'What are you afraid of?' he asked sneeringly. 'Savini's ghost? Or — ' The tall man stopped him, clutching his arm quickly.

'For heaven's sake, don't talk like that!' he said fearfully. 'Let's get on with the job. What do we do first?'

'The library is our immediate objective,' replied the owner of the torch. 'After that we shall see.'

He shuffled towards the staircase, flashing his light above him. The bare boards creaked in protest under their combined weight as they mounted swiftly, the shorter man leading the way and moving with a sureness that spoke of long familiarity with his surroundings. Pausing at a door on the left of the first landing, he gripped the handle and pushed it open. The room beyond was large and oblong, and as he sent the rays of the torch dancing about, it revealed the dusty heaps of books piled everywhere in hopeless confusion — in stacks on the faded carpet; in scattered piles on the tables and chairs; thrust carelessly on the shelves with which the walls were lined. A strong musty smell of old paper and leather bindings greeted them as they entered and closed the door.

'It's not going to be easy to find what we want among all this rubbish!' snarled the man with the claw-like hands, his eyes behind the mask darting quickly about from side to side. 'Did you bring the candles?'

The other nodded and produced them from his pocket.

'Light them and stick them on that table,' was the order. The speaker was rapidly turning over a pile of books on a chair, examining the backs and putting them down again.

'What are you looking for?' asked the tall man as he lighted three candles and stuck them to the large oak table in the centre of the room with melted wax. 'You 'aven't told me yet.'

'We're looking for a book — *Morgan's*

Organic Chemistry, volume two,' snapped his companion shortly.

'A book — ?' said the other in astonishment.

'Yes,' was the snarled reply. 'Don't talk; come and help me to find it, or we shall be here all night.' He pocketed his torch and, stooping, began to look through the scattered volumes on the floor. 'You take the shelves,' he grunted, 'and let me know directly you find it.'

For some time they searched feverishly, while the wind outside rattled at the window-sashes and whined mournfully round the angles of the house, mingling with the thud of each discarded book as it was hastily examined and thrown impatiently down. A sudden draught flickered the candle flames, and the tall man swung round with a startled exclamation.

'What's the matter? Have you found the book?' said the other, looking up quickly.

'No. Look — the door!' The reply came in a voice that trembled. 'I thought you shut it!'

'So I did!'

The black-garbed, stooping figure twisted round. The door that he had closed stood open! Pulling a pistol from his pocket, he shuffled quickly across and peered out into the darkness of the landing, listening intently. There was no sound, only the patter of the rain on a window as the wind sprayed the drops against the glass.

'Must have been the wind,' he muttered, coming back into the room. 'The place is confoundedly draughty.'

He shut the door again, and once more they began their search, though every now and again the tall man shot a nervous glance over his shoulder at the closed door.

Nearly an hour dragged slowly by, and then suddenly, with a cry of exultation, the short, squat figure straightened up, a large green-covered volume clutched in one skinny hand. 'Got it!' he muttered, limping hurriedly over to the table, his companion at his elbow.

Laying the book down, he took from an inside pocket the worn leather wallet that Anthony had found in the hall, and with trembling fingers extracted the sheet of paper and the key.

'Get your notebook and write down what I tell you,' he ordered harshly, and the other, breathing quickly in his excitement, produced a pocket notepad.

With the sheet of jumbled letters and figures before him, the man with the ivory hands began to turn the pages of the book rapidly. At page 101 he stopped. The fifth word in the fourth line was marked with a pencil dot.

'Put down 'seventh', he grunted, and his long, lean forefinger moved to another pencilled word — the eighth in the sixth line. 'Brick,' he read out and the tall man added it to the word he had already scribbled. The other turned several pages and stopped again at 116. In the second line two words — the seventh and the ninth — bore the tiny mark against them, and 'left' and 'staple' were put down beside the others.

Comparing the letters and figures on the sheet with the figures and words in the book, the sinister figure crouching over the table spelt out the message, and at last, with an exclamation of triumph, he closed the heavy volume and flung it into a corner.

'At last!' he cried, tearing the notebook eagerly from the hands of the tall man and swiftly scanning the lines of pencilled writing, 'At last! 'Seventh brick, left staple under bench, laboratory'.' He chuckled hoarsely. 'Come quickly, let us go and collect the fortune that awaits us behind that seventh brick.'

Clutching the key in a claw-like hand, he shuffled to the door, a grotesque, evil figure in that fitful light. 'Bring a candle with you,' he flung back over his shoulder as he hurried out onto the landing, and the other obeyed, never noticing in his excitement that he had jarred the table as he did so, and as a result one of the candles had become dislodged and rolled onto the floor. It remained burning bluely as he followed his companion down the staircase to the hall below.

Turning sharply, the short, squat figure led the way to a door set in the wall immediately behind the stairs. Taking a key from his pocket, he unlocked it, and they entered a large lofty room, the brick walls of which were covered with discoloured diagrams, grime-stained and festooned with cobwebs. The light of the candle which the tall man held was reflected from the collection of glass retorts, beakers, test-tubes, and an assortment of weird-looking instruments which loaded a plain deal table in the centre. One wall was covered with shelves on which stood countless bottles of every shape and size, and over all lay that eternal film of grey dust which seemed to enshroud the whole house like a winding sheet.

'This way. Bring the light over here,' hissed the man with the ivory hands, going over to a long bench that ran underneath the window.

The tall man obeyed and, stooping, held the candle while the squat figure of the other crawled among the litter and dirt beneath the bench and searched along the wall. He found the staple quickly enough, and counting the seventh brick to the left, examined it carefully. In one corner protruded a rusty nail that had been driven in almost to the head, and grasping this in his repulsive-looking fingers, he tugged at it fiercely. It required all his strength to move the brick, for time had almost welded it to the others, but presently he felt it loosen, and a few seconds later he had succeeded in pulling it bodily from the wall.

'Bring the light nearer — nearer to the hole,' he grated breathlessly, and when the other did so, he saw in the orifice that the dislodged brick had revealed a rusty square of metal, in the centre of which was a tiny keyhole.

Panting with excitement and the exertions which his uncomfortable position entailed, he inserted the key. At first it refused to turn either way, for the mechanism of the lock had rusted with long disuse, but putting forth all his strength, he eventually felt it grate round. A sharp jerk of the wrist and the metal plate swung open sideways on a hinge. Feeling about eagerly in the box-like cavity beyond, he brought to light a small object that weighed heavily as he held it between his fingers. It was a little leaden casket and, scrambling to his feet, he set it on the bench and burst into a shrill cackle of delight.

'Behold,' he cried, rubbing his long, skinny hands together in ecstasy, 'a fortune worth two hundred thousand pounds!'

The tall man eyed the casket doubtfully. 'It doesn't seem possible — ' he began, but the other cut him short.

'But it *is* possible — it is a fact!' he exclaimed shrilly. 'That casket contains the most precious substance in the world — radium!' He picked up the little leaden box and dropped it into his pocket. 'Put back that brick!' he ordered harshly, 'and let us get away from here!'

The tall man set the candle on the bench and stooped to obey. As he did so one of the claw-like yellow hands flashed like lightning inside the coat; a knife glittered for a moment in the candlelight, and the next was buried to the hilt between the other's shoulder-blades.

With one choking groan the body sagged forward, gave one convulsive shudder, and lay motionless.

The murderer looked down at it unemotionally except for the eyes, which shone evilly through the slits in the mask. 'You fool!' he muttered contemptuously. 'Did you imagine that I should ever share with you? You've served your purpose, and I have got my just reward.'

'Not yet!' said a gentle voice from the doorway. 'But it won't be long delayed, Shard — it won't be long delayed!'

The man in black swung round with a stifled cry and stared — into the smiling face of Mr. Robert Budd.

13

A Remarkably Dangerous Man

The big superintendent advanced slowly, a long-barrelled Browning covering the cowering figure in black.

'I want you,' he said in the same soft, almost apologetic tone, and when he spoke like that Mr. Budd was most dangerous. 'Put up your hands — quick — right up to the beautiful sky!'

With a little snarling, animal-like noise, the other raised his long arms above his head.

'That's better!' The Rosebud nodded his satisfaction. Keeping his eyes fixed on the man in front of him, he called to someone outside the door. 'Come and run over him and see what he's got in his pockets, will you?'

A figure appeared on the threshold, and as it came into the circle of light cast by the candle, the man in black gave a violent start, for he recognized Anthony Gale, and behind him the white face of Mollie Trayne.

'Didn't expect to see me again, did you?' remarked the reporter pleasantly. 'Thought I was drowned in that death-trap of yours by the river. Well, I wasn't.'

'Damn you!' croaked the man called Shard, his voice choking with the fury that consumed him. 'How did you get away? I suppose it was that interfering policeman!' He glared malignantly at Mr. Budd.

'No, it wasn't me,' said the Rosebud, shaking his head. 'If there's one thing I hate more than the criminal classes, it's taking credit for something I don't deserve. It was a gentleman named Castleton Smith who spoilt your pretty little plan.'

'That's right!' broke in a deep voice from the doorway, and Shard's eyes turned to a fourth figure, a freckled-faced young man who was lounging nonchalantly against the doorpost, smiling cheerfully. 'Alone I did it! I arrived at Anthony's place just in time to see him whisked off in a motor car, having very generously offered to become a special messenger for that occasion only. The whole thing looked so fishy to me that I hung on the back, and when you arrived at that old house by the river, you were carrying an uninvited passenger.

'I didn't know how many of you there might be, so I decided not to butt in all on my lonesome, but went and informed the local police. We were only just in time though. The water was up to Anthony's chin when we found him. I'm afraid we spoilt the party and soured your whole life, old thing.' He tilted his hat further back on his head and grinned.

The man in black muttered something that was unintelligible, and Anthony felt his body trembling with the rage that possessed him as he swiftly ran through his pockets. He unearthed the automatic and the leaden casket and, slipping the former into his own pocket, looked up at the stolid Mr. Budd.

'That's all,' he said. 'What shall I do with this?' He held out the box.

'Keep it for the moment,' said the Rosebud, 'and take off that handkerchief that he's wearing. I should like to look upon his beauty unadorned.'

With a swift jerk, the reporter pulled down the silk mask, revealing a long, deeply lined yellow face distorted with such a diabolical expression of rage that it was scarcely human. The narrow slits of eyes peered out from the taut flesh malevolently, fixing themselves on the stout detective with a look that was evil incarnate.

'Hm, I'm not surprised you wore a mask,' grunted Mr. Budd, and then sternly changing his tone: 'Your name is John Shard, and I arrest you for the murder of your brother, Dr. Emanuel Shard; the murder of Louis Savini; the murder of Jeffrey Tallent; and that poor fellow over there.' He jerked his head towards the still form lying motionless in the shadow of the bench. 'There are several other charges, including the death of a gentleman named Caryll, but these will do to be going on with.' There was a jingle of steel as he withdrew from his pocket a pair of handcuffs and held them out to Anthony. 'Slip these on his wrists — ' he began and was interrupted by a cry from Mollie.

'Tony — look!' she exclaimed fearfully from the doorway. 'The house — it's on fire!'

Startled at the sudden sound of her voice, Mr. Budd involuntarily turned his head, and for a fraction of a second took his eyes off Shard. Almost instantly he remembered, and jerked them back; but that momentary lapse of attention was enough for the murderer. With a tigerish spring, he leapt the intervening space between himself and the stout detective, sending Anthony flying with a powerful blow in his ribs, and gripping the pistol, wrenched it from Mr. Budd's grasp.

The whole action was so quickly carried out that the Scotland Yard man was taken completely by surprise, and before he could recover himself or make any move, he was looking into the muzzle of his own Browning held menacingly in the skinny yellow hand of Shard.

With his thin lips curled in a wolfish snarl, the man in black backed slowly towards the door. 'Keep still, all of you!' he grated viciously. 'I'll blow the first person who moves a finger to hell!'

Still facing them, he crossed the threshold, and Mollie shrank away against the wall, feeling physically sick as he brushed by her. A weird red glow from above flickered spasmodically on his half-crouching figure as he reached the passage, so that he looked like some materialized demon from the underworld.

'You're all very clever,' he snarled, 'but I think the last laugh is with me. Neither do I intend to go empty-handed.' He shot a malevolent glance at the prostrate figure of Anthony. 'I'll trouble you for that leaden box. Quick, throw it over to me! I've no time to waste.'

The words had scarcely left his lips when there came a thundering knock on the front door and, startled, Shard half-swung round in the direction of the sound. As he did so, moving with incredible speed for so large a man, Mr. Budd launched his huge form through the open doorway. There was a fusillade of shots as the murderer fired at him wildly, but luckily the bullets went wide, though Anthony felt the vicious hum of one as it flew past his head, and the next instant the Rosebud and his quarry were struggling in a confused heap on the floor.

The strength of that stunted shape, however, was enormous, for even as Anthony sprang forward to the detective's assistance, Shard succeeded in wrenching himself free and, leaping to his feet, went racing towards the staircase. But he had forgotten Castleton Smith. With a dexterous movement of his foot, that worthy young man tripped him up as he flew past, and with the added impetus of his flight Shard went headlong, falling with a crash on the parquet floor.

Before he could move, Anthony had flung himself on him, and when the panting Mr. Budd succeeded in staggering to his feet, he found Shard lying helpless and handcuffed, with the young reporter leaning against the wall wiping the perspiration from his streaming face and the hall filled with a confused babel of voices emanating from the half-dozen plainclothes men whom Mollie had admitted through the front door.

'We guessed there was something wrong when we saw the flames, sir,' said a tall sergeant, going up to Mr. Budd. 'The whole of the upper part of the house is blazing like a furnace, and we were afraid you might have got trapped.' He looked down at the handcuffed man. 'Is this the fellow, sir?'

'That is the fellow,' answered the Rosebud carefully. 'Take him along, Sergeant, and keep a strong guard over him, for he is a remarkably dangerous man!'

★   ★   ★

In spite of the efforts of the hastily summoned fire brigade, it was impossible to save Whispering Beeches from the devouring flames. The old house with its panelled walls and oak beams burned like tinder, and when dawn broke greyly there was nothing left of the gloomy, ill-omened mansion except a heap of smouldering blackened ruins and part of the wall that reared its solitary bulk, a silent epitaph to that which was no more, against the rapidly lighting sky.

The stout Mr. Budd did not wait for the end, but accompanied his prisoner back to Cannon Row, which adjoins Scotland Yard, and in a bare and cheerless cell subjected him to a close examination.

It was a long time before Shard could be persuaded to break the sullen silence which he had maintained since his capture, but eventually, realizing that everything was hopeless, he did so, and the story that he told tore the last veil from the mystery surrounding Sinister House.

It was the following evening before the Rosebud found time to satisfy the curiosity of an impatient Anthony, and then in the cosy sitting room of Mollie Trayne's flat he unfolded the sequence of events which had led up to and formed part of the strange drama that ended with the holocaust that destroyed its setting.

Everybody will remember the full-page article which appeared under the name of Anthony Gale in the *Courier*, and which caused the taciturn Mr. Downer to smile for the first and last time in his life. So it is only necessary to touch on the salient points in the story that the Rosebud recounted as they sat round Mollie's cheerful fire and listened to the stout detective's laborious sentences.

'John Shard, as you already know, was Dr. Emanuel's brother,' he began. 'A careless nurse who dropped him when he was a year old was the cause of his physical deformity. Whether this also affected him mentally is impossible to say, but from an early age he developed criminal tendencies, and was always in trouble of one sort or another. Before he was twenty-four he had served several short sentences for minor robberies in America, and in spite of his elder brother's efforts to reform him he went from bad to worse. Eventually, having made New York too hot to hold him, he disappeared, and his brother lost all trace of him.'

The Rosebud paused, took a cigar from his pocket, looked at the girl for permission to smoke, and lit it carefully. 'According to his own account,' he continued after two or three slow puffs, 'he spent several years in China and then drifted to South Africa. Here he got mixed up with illicit diamond-buying and was sentenced to five years in Pretoria Central, afterwards being transferred to the Breakwater.

'About the same time as Dr. Shard arrived in England, his brother succeeded in escaping from the Breakwater. Penniless and hunted — how he evaded capture is a mystery to me — he saw one day a short paragraph in a newspaper mentioning his brother's whereabouts and decided to seek him out and obtain help. By devious routes he worked his way to London, and almost the first person he met on his arrival was Louis Savini, an international crook whom he had known intimately in America. Savini was working at the time with Tallent, who fenced the proceeds of the various robberies carried out by the gang they jointly controlled. Tallent had learnt that, for the purposes of his experiments, Dr. Shard had in his possession a quantity of radium, close on two hundred thousand pounds' worth, which had been loaned to him by the State College of Research in America, and for some time Tallent had been trying to devise a plan by which he and Savini could get this valuable substance into their own hands.

'Dr. Shard was a nervous man and careful inquiries had elicited the fact that not even his secretary, Caryll, knew where he kept his stock of the rare salt, the experiments for which it was used being carried out by the doctor alone behind locked doors. He had, however, taken the precaution of setting down in cipher form the place where it was hidden, and had told Caryll that the key was to be found in *Morgan's Organic Chemistry* volume two. The cipher itself he carried about with him in a leather wallet. He had suffered for a long time with his heart, and it was only if anything should happen to him that the secretary was instructed to return the radium to the College of Research where it belonged. These precautions seem, I'll admit, rather ridiculous, but you must take into account the fact that he was undoubtedly eccentric, that the radium was of great value and was, moreover, only loaned to him. To cut a long story short, Tallent and Savini learned these facts — except the fact that Caryll knew the key to the cipher — by getting Selton, who was a member of their gang, a job as gardener at Whispering Beeches.

'When Savini found out that Shard was the doctor's brother, he took him into their confidence and outlined a plan which he and Tallent had previously formed and were going to carry out on their own. It was simple in the extreme.

'Doctor Shard was in the habit of working far into the night. Armed with a duplicate key to the laboratory and the back door — which of course Tallent, who let the property, had in his possession — Savini and Selton were to take him by surprise late one night and force him to reveal where the radium was kept. On the night when Dr. Shard was murdered the scheme was carried out, the only alteration being that they substituted John Shard for Selton, but Tallent and Savini had not reckoned on the fits of demoniacal rage that occasionally took possession of the hunchback, and this was their undoing.

'They found the doctor in his laboratory, and Savini, according to plan, waited in the hall while Shard went in to his brother. It was because they thought that Shard was less likely to give the alarm if he was suddenly confronted by his own brother that he had been chosen instead of Selton. Dr. Shard was so furious at the sight of his brother that he threatened all sorts of things if he didn't go immediately, and finally he aroused the other's temper to such a degree that John Shard stabbed him. His rage subsided directly he realized what he had done, but it was too late. His brother was already dead, and with him had died the secret of where the radium was hidden.

Shard called in Savini, and they held a hurried consultation. It was useless to try and extract information from a dead man, so they made a swift search of the laboratory, but without finding what they sought. Savini remembered the cipher, and in the doctor's pocket they found the leather wallet containing it and the small key. But without Caryll it was useless — he alone knew where the solution to that jumble was to be found.

'Shard and Savini had decided to give it up and get away while they were safe when Caryll, who had been out late, returned and caught them. Before he had time, however, to give the alarm, Shard knocked him senseless, and it was then he suggested that they should kidnap him and make him reveal the secret of the cipher message. They took him to an old house by the river at Wraysbury, which belonged to Tallent, and where Shard had been living — the same, by the way, where you and Miss Trayne nearly met your deaths — and here Shard tried by every evil means in his power to force Caryll to speak. What tortures the unfortunate man went through we can, knowing Shard, imagine, and at last he told the hunchback what he wanted to know. But the strain he had undergone during the intervening period proved too much for him. He died and Shard buried the body in the garden.

'The position was now this — Savini and Tallent had the cipher and Shard had the key to it, for he had been alone when

Caryll finally spoke, and neither was of use without the other. Knowing this, Shard refused to part with his knowledge unless he received two-thirds of the proceeds instead of one-third, which had been originally agreed upon. The situation developed into a feud between Shard and Tallent, which lasted for nearly three years, while each was trying to get the information required from the other. At last Shard managed to lure Savini into Sinister House, killed him and secured the wallet which he afterwards lost during his fight with you.'

Mr. Budd drew a long breath and leaned back to the imminent peril of Mollie's chair. 'The rest you know,' he said.

'There's one thing I don't understand,' declared Anthony after a pause. 'What part did Mollie play in all this?'

The Rosebud smiled and looked across at the woman with a wink. 'Shall I tell him?' he asked. 'Or will you?'

'You tell him,' answered Mollie quickly.

The superintendent cleared his throat. 'When the death of Shard became known

155

in America,' he said, 'the State College of Research became anxious about their radium and got in touch with the American police, who communicated with Scotland Yard. We did our best, but had to cable eventually that we could find no trace of it. The president of the college, however, wasn't satisfied, and enlisted the aid of Pinkerton's, and — 'The Rosebud stopped and chuckled. ' — and there you are!' he added.

A light suddenly dawned in Anthony's brain. 'You mean — ?' he almost shouted, rising to his feet.

'They sent over the best detective I have ever met,' said Mr. Budd. 'She ought to have all the credit, for it was she who found out that John Shard was in England, and discovered his and Savini's connections with the case. It was while she was following Savini on the night of his murder that Shard chloroformed her. Luckily he thought she was only a friend of Savini's. If he'd guessed the truth, I don't suppose she would be alive now.'

'I spent most of my time following you about,' put in Mollie, smiling up into

Anthony's amazed eyes.

'Then the green car was yours?' he stuttered dazedly.

'Yes, I brought it with me from New York. It's a wonderful machine.'

'You're a wonderful woman,' said the Rosebud admiringly.

'She is!' declared Anthony fervently.

'I think I'll go and have a look at that new florist's in Regent Street,' remarked Mr. Budd softly, and discreetly withdrew.

Flowers for the Dead

The easiest thing that Mr. William Predergast ever did was to murder his wife.

He had contemplated this step for several months, spending many a long evening while she sat opposite him engrossed in her interminable knitting, working out various elaborate and complicated plans. Curiously enough, when he actually killed her he used a means that was simple and crude.

When he awoke on that Sunday morning he had no thoughts of murder in his mind. It was a combination of trivial circumstances that forced him to the conclusion that this was the ideal time to put his long-cherished intention into practice.

The first of these occurred at breakfast, when his wife announced her intention of going up to London that afternoon to spend a few days with an old school friend who lived in Kensington. Mr. Predergast was not surprised at this sudden decision. His wife had a habit of keeping her plans to herself until the last moment. Nor was it the first time she had gone to stay for a few days with her friend.

The second circumstance was that on a Sunday there were no trains from the small station that served the village, so that she would have to begin her journey from the busy Junction three miles away.

It was the third circumstance, taken in conjunction with these two, that decided him.

The Predergasts lived in a small cottage on the outskirts of a little village in Kent. It was a pretty place with a tiny garage big enough to house Mr. Predergast's ancient car and a fair-sized garden, which was Mrs. Predergast's particular joy. From January to December it was gay with bloom and owed its geometrical neatness to her untiring efforts, assisted by the bi-weekly visits of an old man from the village. At the present moment a thinning patch in the lawn was receiving attention. An oblong of grass had been neatly removed, and rolls of fresh turf were stacked beside this, ready to be laid down. This bare patch of earth in the otherwise smooth surface of the lawn was the deciding factor that was to turn Mr. Predergast from a murderer in intention to a murderer in fact.

Mrs. Predergast packed her suitcase immediately after breakfast, informed her husband that he was to be ready to take her to the Junction in time to catch the four-thirty-six train to London, and went out in her old tweed suit to spend the rest of the morning gardening.

Mr. Predergast, a little excited, but not unduly so, completed his hastily formed plans. At eleven o'clock he made coffee and called his wife in from the garden. She came, unsuspecting that this was to be her last moment alive, stripped off her old gardening gloves, and sat down at the kitchen table.

Mr. Predergast set a cup of steaming coffee before her, picked up the wooden mallet which he had placed in readiness, and stepping behind her chair, hit her twice over the head with all his force. She fell across the table with scarcely a sound. The coffee cup broke and the coffee swilled over the table and dripped onto the tiled floor.

Mr. Predergast saw that there was very little blood. He buried the body, just as it was in the old tweed suit, in the oblong patch in the lawn, carefully laid down the fresh turf, and rolled it several times with the garden roller. Then he went back to the kitchen and tidied it up. The suitcase and its contents he destroyed in the boiler, making sure that every scrap was completely burned.

When he had finished he sat down for a rest and a smoke. A wonderful sense of freedom filled him. No longer was he a slave. At last, after twenty long and weary years, he was free. Free to do as he liked and go where he liked . . .

Of course there was an inquiry. Mr. Predergast started it himself. On the following morning he rang up the friend with whom his wife had contemplated staying. He was very properly surprised and alarmed when he was told that she was not there and had never arrived. The police came and listened to all he had to tell them, went away and came again with more questions but no news of the missing woman.

The weeks merged into months. The old gardener from the village continued to come in twice a week to keep the garden tidy. He cut and rolled the lawn and there was no longer any sign of the oblong patch under which the body of Mrs. Predergast lay.

The police inquiry into her disappearance was still going on, but the general opinion was that she had left her husband and gone off somewhere with some man or other. Mr. Predergast fostered this theory.

In the spring, Mr. Predergast decided to take a holiday. The strain had been severe and he felt in need of a change. He no longer had to consult anyone about his movements. He was free.

He shut up the cottage and went to a secluded town on the coast where he spent, for the first time in his life, a peaceful and enjoyable holiday.

On the day he was due to return home

he came down to breakfast and was accosted in the hotel lobby by a thick-set man whose profession was unmistakable.

'You are William Predergast?' asked the man curtly.

With a sudden sick feeling in the pit of his stomach, Mr. Predergast agreed that he was.

'I'm Detective-Inspector Webley of the Criminal Investigation Department, New Scotland Yard,' announced the thick-set man. 'I'm taking you into custody for the murder of your wife, Agnes Predergast. I must warn you that anything you say may be used in evidence . . .

'But . . . I don't understand,' began Mr. Predergast. 'My wife disappeared . . . '

'That was your story,' broke in the thick-set man. 'But she didn't go very far, did she?'

'You're making a terrible mistake,' said Mr. Predergast, moistening his suddenly dry lips with the tip of his tongue.

'If I am it can be corrected at your trial,' retorted the detective. 'I don't want to make a scene here. If you'll come quietly . . . '

'But I've no more idea what happened to my wife than you have,' protested Mr. Predergast.

'Then you must have a very good idea,' answered Webley. 'We dug up the body of your wife yesterday — where you buried it. Under the lawn at your cottage.'

'What made you look there?' asked Mr. Predergast.

'Just something you overlooked,' said the inspector. 'It's a queer thing, but it's my experience that you people always do overlook something. It's a lucky thing for us. That's how we catch you.'

'I still don't understand,' said Mr. Predergast.

'You didn't search your wife's pockets before you buried her, did you?' said Webley.

Mr. Predergast remembered that he hadn't. He didn't say so. He just stared at the other in perplexity.

'If you had,' went on the inspector, 'you'd probably have got away with it. We didn't suspect murder, you know. We thought she'd gone away of her own free will for some reason or other. But the finding of the body put a different complexion on it, of course. That was as good as if you'd signed a confession.'

He waited for a moment but Mr. Predergast was silent.

'When you buried the body of your wife,' he continued after a pause, 'the pockets of the tweed suit she was wearing were full of tulip bulbs. They grew up and bloomed in the *middle of the lawn*. When your gardener tried to dig 'em up he found — how they'd got there.'

Mr. Predergast, grey-faced and hopeless, stared at him.

Design for Libel

I hadn't seen Gretley for nearly two years when I ran across him that morning in a little teashop off the strand.

I had come up to London to keep an appointment, but I was a bit early and decided to fill in the time with a coffee. The first person I saw as I entered the teashop was Gretley. He was sitting at a table in the corner, smoking a cigarette and staring gloomily at the empty cup in front of him. He looked shabby. Life hadn't, I thought, been treating him too well.

Gretley, in the past, had always been full of get-rich-quick schemes but, judging from his appearance, none of them had done him much good.

I went over and sat down in the vacant chair opposite him. 'Hello,' I greeted him cheerfully. 'You're the last person I expected to see.'

He looked up quickly. 'Good lor', it's

Hatherway,' he exclaimed. 'I didn't expect to see you, either. I thought you were abroad.'

'Got back last week,' I said. 'Have another coffee and tell me all about yourself.'

He made a grimace. 'That won't take long,' he retorted. 'I'll have the coffee, though.'

I ordered two coffees from the waitress, offered Gretley a cigarette, and lit one myself. 'What have you been doing since I last saw you?' I asked. 'Any of the great schemes materialised?'

'Do I look as if they had?' he demanded bitterly. 'Don't talk to me of schemes. If it hadn't been for a scheme I shouldn't be like this — broke to the wide and utterly fed up.'

'Things pretty bad, eh?' I said sympathetically. In the old days Gretley and I had been rather good friends. 'I'm sorry.'

'They couldn't be much worse,' he answered. 'But you're wasting your sympathy. It's entirely my own fault. If I hadn't been such a flaming fool . . . '

He broke off as the waitress came over

with our coffee. When she had gone again, he went on abruptly: 'Look here, I'll tell you about it if you can spare the time.'

'I've nothing to do for half an hour,' I said. 'Go ahead.'

'It'll be a relief to tell someone,' he grunted, stirring his coffee rapidly. 'You remember I used to write a bit? Had an idea that I was going to blossom into a best-seller and make a fortune? Well, I *did* write a novel, and after one or two rejections got it taken by Toogood and Smith — small advance and royalties. It didn't do very well — sold just about enough to cover the advance — but the reviews were quite good. If I'd stuck at it I'd probably be making a pretty good living now instead of . . . Well, instead of this.' He looked down at his frayed coat sleeve. 'But I always wanted to get money quickly,' he went on. 'The plodding business was never in my line and I was too impatient to wait. Toogood's had agreed to take another book, and I was wondering how I could force the sales of this into really big figures and clear up a packet quickly, when I met a man called Pettleton — and that was the beginning of the trouble.'

He gulped down half his coffee quickly. 'Do you know anything about the law of libel?' he asked.

'Not very much,' I answered.

'Well, simplified a bit it's this,' said Gretley. 'If an author uses an existing person's name in a novel and makes the fictional character unpleasant or a bad type, the real person can sue the author, the publisher, and the printer for libel and get substantial damages. It doesn't matter whether the author has ever heard of the real person or not; the mere accidental use of an existing person's name is sufficient. Is that clear?'

I nodded. 'It seems rather a risky business to write a book at all,' I remarked.

'It is,' said Gretley. 'Luckily it's very rarely taken advantage of. Even the fact that the publisher prints a notice in the front of the book that all the characters are fictitious doesn't make any difference. The law of libel operates just the same.

However, to get on with the story. This fellow, Pettleton, knew all about the law; and one night, when I was explaining how I was trying to find some scheme that would put over my next book in a big way, he quietly put forward his suggestion.

' 'I take it, Gretley,' he said, 'that what you are after is to get hold of a large sum of money quickly?' I agreed that that was the idea. 'Well, I can tell you how to do it,' he went on, 'that is, of course, provided that you don't care for your reputation as an author.' I hadn't any reputation worth speaking about and I told him so. 'Very well, then,' he said. 'Why don't you put *me* in your next book? Use my name, make the character a thoroughly bad one — an unpleasant chap without a redeeming feature. I'll sue for libel and we'll split the damages.'

' 'What good is that going to do me?' I demanded. 'I haven't any money to pay the damages.'

'Pettleton laughed. 'My dear chap, you don't understand,' he said. 'If you haven't any money the *publishers* have to pay ... ' He explained that the publishers, printers, and myself would be sued jointly and whoever had the money would have to fork out. The law wasn't concerned who paid. 'The damages should be pretty heavy,' said Pettleton. 'I've a fairly good reputation in my business and I can easily fake up proof that the publication of the book has affected me adversely.'

'To cut a long story short,' said Gretley, 'I agreed. There didn't seem much I could lose. Toogood and Smith, of course, wouldn't have anything more to do with me, but I wasn't making anything out of them as it was. I wrote the book. I made Pettleton the most appalling scoundrel you could imagine. A fortnight after the book was published, Pettleton issued his writ for libel. There was a tremendous to-do. I was sent for and soundly berated. Offers were made to Pettleton to settle the matter out of court, but he turned them all down. The case came up for trial and Pettleton produced witnesses to prove that his business had suffered from the book, and not only his business but his private life, too.

'The judge was obviously on his side from the start. After two days' hearing and a great deal of publicity, Pettleton won his case. He was awarded ten thousand pounds in damages and costs. Toogood and Smith paid up, though nobody could say they looked pleasant about it.' Gretley finished the rest of his coffee.

'And you got five thousand?' I said.

Gretley shook his head. 'I got nothing,' he replied. 'Not a cent, not a sausage.'

'But . . . ' I began.

'Pettleton collared the lot,' interrupted Gretley disgustedly. 'I couldn't do a darned thing about it. I couldn't say it had been a put-up job between us, could I? I should have found myself in the jug for fraudulent conspiracy.'

'Well, that's what it was, wasn't it?' I said.

'Meaning,' said Gretley, 'that I got what I deserved? Well, I suppose you're right. But I do begrudge having to pay that swine Pettleton ten thousand pounds.'

'But you didn't,' I pointed out. 'It was

Toogood and Smith who did that.'

Gretley stubbed out the butt of his cigarette viciously. 'Did they heck!' he exclaimed. 'They paid it out in the first place, but I'm paying it now. That first book I wrote for them suddenly began to sell. It sold in the thousands. It's *still* selling. And I'm not getting a penny out of it. Toogood and Smith are taking all the royalties to repay that ten thousand pounds.'

The Weir

I was surprised when I heard from Sinclair that Redmayne was in hospital, and even more surprised when I learned that he was there as the result of an accident with his boat.

It appeared that he had taken the wrong side of the river in the dusk, where it was divided by an island, and instead of entering the lock cut, as he must have intended, he had driven straight into the weir, smashing up the boat and himself pretty badly. The whole thing seemed queer to me. Redmayne is an experienced waterman. I don't suppose there is anybody who knows the Thames better than he; every inch of it from Teddington to Letchlade. He'd been cruising up and down the river for years in that fast launch of his, and there isn't a reach or a backwater that isn't as familiar to him as a back garden is to you or me. I was puzzled therefore to know how he could have come to make such a mistake even in the dusk. There's always a notice put up by the Thames Conservancy showing the way to all locks, and usually another clearly marked 'Danger' at the entrance to a backwater leading into a weir and, as I say, Redmayne knew the river.

There was another thing too. He must have been going at a dickens of a speed to have smashed the launch as he had. One of the most stringent rules laid down by the Conservancy is that no power-driven vessel should be permitted to make more than a nine-inch wash, and you can't go very fast and conform to that! It was incredible to me how Redmayne had managed it, and although Sinclair said he was rather touchy on the subject, and refused to go into any details about it, I was determined to satisfy my curiosity if possible.

He was in a private room at the cottage hospital when I went to see him, and although he had broken his right leg, severely sprained his left wrist, and injured his head, he didn't look too bad. There was no doubt that he was pleased to see me. He put down the book he was reading when the nurse showed me in, and stretched out his right hand.

'I've been hoping you'd come, Thorndyke,' he said. 'I thought most likely you would when Sinclair told you what had happened. I was going to send you a note today if you hadn't. There's some whisky and cigarettes on that table over there. Help yourself and sit down.'

I poured myself a drink, took a cigarette, and sat down on the chair by the bed. 'You seem to have got yourself pretty badly damaged,' I said. 'How did you manage it?'

'Didn't Sinclair tell you?' he asked quickly.

I nodded. 'Yes, but I still don't understand how an expert river man like you could have made such a stupid mistake.'

'We all make mistakes,' he broke in, 'even the best of us. I'll have a spot of whisky if you'll give it me. Not much whisky and plenty of soda.'

I wondered as I mixed the drink whether that was the explanation. Had Redmayne been drunk when he drove the launch into the weir? That seemed the only way to account for it, and it would explain why, as Sinclair had said, he was rather touchy about talking about it.

All the same, it wasn't like Redmayne. I'd known him for years and he'd always been the most abstemious chap. Fond of a glass of beer in the right company, but that was all. I gave him the whisky and he sipped it, looking at me thoughtfully. Although he looked fairly well, considering his injuries, there was something different about him. It wasn't anything very marked; a kind of illusive expression that lurked behind his eyes. There was perplexity and a trace of fear.

That's not really a very good description of it. But it is a difficult thing to set down in words, like trying to describe a perfume or a taste. It may have been the result of the shock, the memory of the moment when he'd known that he was going to crash into the weir. I thought it better not to refer to the accident again for a bit. It obviously disturbed and upset him.

If I was going to learn any more about

it, it would be wiser to approach the subject more delicately. I began therefore to talk about things and people that I thought would interest him. He responded at once, and for perhaps twenty minutes there was an ebb and flow of light gossip between us, you know the kind of thing. Then we began to exhaust our topics of conversation, and there were short silences of varying length while we cast around in our minds for fresh ones. It was during one of these that Redmayne made an odd remark.

'Would you call me a fanciful man, Thorndyke?' he asked seriously, while looking at me very intently.

'No,' I answered, a little surprised at the question. 'Distinctly hard-headed and practical.'

'I always thought so too,' he agreed. 'In fact I've always rather prided myself on possessing just those qualities.'

He stopped, and I could see he was trying to make up his mind about something and wasn't finding it very easy. There was still a little whisky and soda left in his glass and he drained it quickly, looking into the empty glass for a moment and then up at me.

'It wasn't an accident,' he said suddenly. 'Going into that weir, I mean.'

'Good God!' I exclaimed, thoroughly startled. 'Do you mean that you deliberately . . . '

'No! No!' he interrupted quickly. 'That's not it at all. It's a queer story and you probably won't believe a word of it, but I'm going to tell it to you all the same. You've got to promise though that you won't repeat it to a soul. I don't want to have people doubting my sanity. That's why I've kept my mouth shut up until now.'

I gave him the promise readily.

'Well then,' said Redmayne, 'I'll begin at the beginning, and I warn you again that although you won't believe it, what I am going to tell you is a plain statement of what happened. I'm adding no trimmings. Nothing but the actual facts.'

He paused for a long breath and then he continued. 'I'm fond of pottering about the river in my launch, as you know. I suppose I ought to say *was*, because I feel doubtful if I shall ever be again. And I planned a fortnight's trip just chugging along peacefully with no particular objective in view except to do as I liked. A spot of fishing, a bit of reading, an evening spent in one or two of my favourite village pubs; the ideal holiday in my opinion. I stocked the boat with a good supply of canned food and a primus so that I could be independent of hotels if I wanted to; blankets and bedding, fishing gear, a dozen or so new books, and a couple of tins of tobacco, and set off.

'The weather was perfect and looked like remaining so. The upper reaches of the Thames beyond Windsor are the more lovely to my mind, and I spent the first two or three days cruising along steadily, and only stopping for a meal and a short rest. At night I put into the bank when I spotted a pleasant-looking place to moor, and slept like a top, lulled by the restful sound of the water lapping against the boat.

'In the morning as soon as the sun was up I took a dip in the river, shaved, cooked my breakfast, and then I tidied up the boat and smoked a pipe and was off again. I felt as fit as a fiddle and was thoroughly enjoying myself. The engine was running sweetly, and I was looking forward to a completely trouble-free two weeks.'

Redmayne stopped and asked me to give him a little soda water, which I did. When he had taken a sip or two he went on. 'I had decided to make for Cliveden Reach, which is by far the most beautiful stretch of the river, and idle between it and Sonning. I never got as far, as you are aware. On the fourth evening after I had started, I was cruising along slowly looking for a likely place to moor up for the night, when I remembered that a short distance ahead on the left-hand bank there was an old house that had been empty for years.

'It was a big, rambling sort of place in the last stages of decay, and rapidly falling to pieces. The grounds were full of weeds, and well wooded; they ran right down to the water. I'd often thought on previous occasions that it would be a good spot to put in. But I had never done so. The place was private property of course, and strictly speaking I had no right to moor there at all.

'But it was more secluded than the tow-path, and I couldn't see that I should be causing much harm if I tied up there just for the night. Anyway, I decided to do so.

'When I came within sight of the place, I turned the prow of the launch towards the bank and nosed cautiously inshore. The river was quite deep, right up to the old rotting campshedding, and there would have been plenty of water for much bigger craft than mine. In a few minutes I was snugly moored up close to the remains of an old diving board and setting about preparing my supper. By the time I had eaten it, the kettle was boiling on the primus, and I made myself some tea.

'The sun had set some time ago but it was still fairly light and very quiet — the kind of unnatural quietness that precedes a thunderstorm, although there was no sign of anything of that sort. Nothing stirred. Not even a bird in the thick-growing trees.

'I drank my tea and smoked my pipe in supreme enjoyment. I don't remember feeling so completely contented. It began to grow dark, and as the darkness increased I felt the beginning of a queer uneasiness. It didn't come upon me all at once, but stealthily in direct ratio with the fading light. It was an uncomfortable feeling and I could find nothing to account for it. I decided that the best thing to do was to go to bed, so I started to unpack my bedding. As I moved about the boat it rocked gently, and it was this that left me quite unprepared for what happened next. I was stooping down with my back to the river when suddenly I heard a woman's voice say softly: '*Hello.*'

'Thoroughly surprised and startled, I turned round. A girl was clinging to the side of the launch, smiling up at me. She was a very lovely girl with dark, wavy hair, with the water trickling off her bare shoulders. '*Hello,*' she said again. All I could do was to stare at her foolishly. She laughed and her teeth gleamed whitely in the deepening dusk.

' 'Where . . . where do you come from?' I stammered.

' 'I've been swimming,' she answered. 'I love swimming. What a beautiful launch. I used to have one almost exactly like it. Can I come on board?'

'I concluded that she must have swum across from the towpath or from some house along the bank. Although I was rather annoyed at this disturbance of my privacy, I didn't want to appear churlish, so I helped her to scramble over the side; and when she stood dripping little pools of water on the bottom of the boat I saw she was wearing a rather old-fashioned sort of bathing dress.

'"What are you doing here?' she asked, and I explained I had moored up there for the night. 'You're not allowed to moor up here you know,' she said. 'This is private property.'

'I told her I knew that, but since there was nobody living there I didn't see what harm I was doing. She made no reply to this, and I decided that I definitely didn't like her. All that increasing uneasiness, which I had experienced before she put in an appearance, seemed to gather and concentrate, and she was the focal point.

'I suggested, perhaps rather curtly, that she ought to be getting back to wherever she came from. 'There's plenty of time,' she said. 'I want you to take me for a trip in this lovely boat. You will, won't you?' She was looking at me with her head a little on one side and a faint mocking smile curving her full lips. 'Please.' She stretched out a slim, very white hand and laid it on my arm.

'The touch sent a cold shiver of intense disgust through me. I wanted, and I fully intended, to refuse point blank, but instead I found myself agreeing. 'I knew you would,' she said softly, and I noticed that her voice had grown thick and treacly as though she was labouring under a sudden intense emotion. 'It will be lovely, so very lovely.'

'I started the engine and cast off. I didn't want to but I couldn't help myself. It was as if my willpower had been completely sapped away. We moved out into midstream and headed upriver. It was almost quite dark now, as dark as it would get, and I switched on the navigation lights. The sky was clear, a vast dome of bluish-green, with here and there a faint star. The houses on either side were black uneven strips with shadows that reached far out into the still water. The girl stood by my side and I could hear her breathing quickly above the soft purr of the engine. 'Let me take the wheel,' she said huskily after a minute or two.

'Again my instinct warned me, but I was incapable of obeying it. She took my place and I stood beside her. Her hand touched the throttle and the launch began to gather speed. I watched the prow rise higher and higher as the stern settled down firmly in the water. A white-topped wall of hissing, bubbling water curved up and away on either side. A wash divided behind us into two great creamy waves. You know what the launch could do all-out, Thorndyke — you've been in her with me over the measured mile at Chelsea — and she was all-out now.

'Close ahead of us I could see the looming black bulk of the island with the narrow entrance of the lock cut on one side and the wider entrance to the backwater on the other. I expected the girl to slow down and steer for the cut, but she did neither. She drove straight for the backwater and the weir. I shouted to her but she only laughed exultantly. Her head was thrown back and her dark hair rippled in the breeze. I wondered why I had thought her lovely, for she wasn't lovely now.

'Her eyes were wild, and her lips were curled back over her white teeth in a horrible snarling smile. I had never seen such an expression of triumphant evil before, and I hope to God I never shall again. I tried to move and drag her away from the wheel, but I couldn't. I was as helpless as though I'd been bound hand and foot. I could see the long line of the weir just in front, and I shouted and screamed but my throat was dry from fear, and all that came out was a rasping whisper. The girl turned her face towards me and burst into a peal of horrible laughter. And then we struck the weir!'

Redmayne's hand was shaking and his face was damp as he drank what was left of his soda water. 'That's the story,' he said. 'I don't expect you to believe it. But you can understand why I kept my mouth shut.'

'What happened to the girl?' I asked.

He looked at me. 'I don't know,' he said slowly. 'I don't know. You'll think me mad, I suppose, but there was nobody at the wheel when we struck the weir. Nobody!'

The old lock-keeper who had pulled Redmayne out of the river and saved his life was only too willing to talk about it. I guessed that it had proved a profitable topic of conversation ever since.

'Can't understand how it could have happened, sir,' he said, shaking his head. 'Not to an experienced gentleman like Mr. Redmayne. You've known him for a good many years, and he's been through this lock time and time again. Now, if it had been one of these here people what hires boats for a couple of weeks . . . ' He spat contemptuously.

'Even they don't have accidents like that,' I said, and he agreed.

'No,' he remarked. 'The only other accident of that kind that I can remember was over twenty year ago. It happened 'ere too. That was a girl, and when she smashed into the weir she was dead drunk. Drowned, she were.'

'Oh? Who was she?' I asked as casually as I could.

'Now let me see, sir,' he said, wrinkling his forehead. 'She lived in the big 'ouse down the reach. It's empty now, been empty ever since. Fast piece of goods. Always giving parties and kicking up a rare din. Come through this lock in her launch they would, screaming and shouting, and as drunk as lords. Now, that's it sir, Lady Margaret Downley. That was 'er name. Her husband had divorced 'er and it was generally supposed she weren't no better than she should be. Crashed 'er launch into this 'ere weir one night just like Mr. Redmayne. Only she was so drunk she didn't know what she was doing.'

I left him soon afterwards with a substantial tip, and as I walked away down the towpath to my car, I wondered. Did this explain Redmayne's queer experience? If it did, how did one explain the explanation? Perhaps there are some things that can't be explained.

THE END

THE FACELESS ONES
GRIM DEATH
MURDER IN MANUSCRIPT
THE GLASS ARROW
THE THIRD KEY
THE ROYAL FLUSH MURDERS
THE SQUEALER
MR. WHIPPLE EXPLAINS
THE SEVEN CLUES
THE CHAINED MAN
THE HOUSE OF THE GOAT
THE FOOTBALL POOL MURDERS
THE HAND OF FEAR
SORCERER'S HOUSE
THE HANGMAN
THE CON MAN
MISTER BIG
THE JOCKEY
THE SILVER HORSESHOE
THE TUDOR GARDEN MYSTERY
THE SHOW MUST GO ON

Other titles in the
Linford Mystery Library:

MURDERS GALORE

Richard A. Lupoff

Murders Galore is a collection of six stories that range through time and place from a World War Two military post, to a Midwestern industrial city, to a boys' vacation camp, to a transcontinental streamliner. The macabre methods and motives involved are as varied as the venues, but the result in each case is — *murder*! Beginning with *The Square Root of Dead*, in which a doomed mathematics professor devises, in his final moments, an ingenious way to identify his killer . . .